Wrecking Bernadette

ALSO BY DANIELLE GRAINGER

THE DENTON HEIGHTS SERIES
Under Her Wing (Book 1)
The Shasti and Madison Story

In Her Cage (Book 2)
The Jaleesa and Tina Story

Within Her Grasp (Book 3)
The Marta and Shanice Story

By Her Command (Book 4)
The Rowena and Minjung Story

Toward Her Passion (Book 5)
The Rikki Carmichael Story

THE BERNADETTE SERIES
Wrecking Bernadette (Book One)

(S)mothering Bernadette (Book Two)

Becoming Bernadette (Book Three)

Desiring Bernadette (Book Four)

Loving Bernadette (Book Five)

WRECKING Bernadette

BOOK ONE IN THE BERNADETTE SERIES

DANIELLE GRAINGER

Paperback ISBN   978-1-953734-14-3

Revised Edition 2021

9 8 7 6 5 4 3 2 1

Cover design by Sarah (Forcoverservice)

Published by:
Bibi Books Publishing Company, LLC

Dedication

This work is dedicated to those practicing safe, sane, consensual, honest, and trusting BDSM.

Acknowledgments

I want to thank the amazing people who helped me understand the BDSM world and its infinite possibilities.

Thank you to those who taught me that BDSM relationships are based on mutual respect and trust. Miss A, GBoo, and Miss S have shown me what true classy dominance looks like in their own ways. Thank you for contributing to my ever-growing understanding.

Table of Contents

Chapter One

Free

I had to move out, but that's okay. Mostly. There are plusses. One big plus is that I can finally get off whenever I want and make as much noise as I want. I don't have to hide, and I don't have to deny myself any longer. I have my own apartment and live there by myself. Having been denied sex from Jen for so long, I feel like I'm making up for lost time. Jen and I were together for four years and stopped having sex after two. Why? Who knows. Lesbian bed death, maybe? I still wanted sex. She didn't, apparently.

The sex with her hadn't been bad. Not that it was good. I mean, okay, it was terrible. At first, I thought we were both satisfied customers, but I think she just got bored with me after a while. I would create these great fantasies in my head so that I could cum fast. But that isn't the kind of connection I want with a life partner. Thank God we hadn't gotten married or anything like that.

For the last couple of years of our relationship, I sneaked orgasms because it was easier than trying to get her to touch me. She even made fun of me if I tried to get her interested in sex. So, I found myself stroking my clit any chance I got, in the shower or after she fell asleep. She had this particular way of breathing that told me she was sleeping, and then my fingers would fly to my nub, and I'd stroke myself until I came. Sometimes stroking my clit wasn't enough. I needed my fingers inside to get off but doing that was always risky. One time she woke up just as I was cresting, and I had to stop. When she asked me what I was doing, I lied and said I was massaging a leg cramp. "Oh," she said and rolled over.

But now, because I live alone, I don't have to sneak orgasms, and when I climax, I can finally cry out as loud as I want to. Well, not too loud. I do have neighbors on the one side and neighbors below me. My music covers it. I hope.

Through careful Internet searching, I've homed in on a website with a good lesbian porn collection that at least tries to cater to real-live lesbians like me. And I can't believe I'm saying this, but I now have a favorite porn star. Can you believe it? Me? Dr. Bernadette Garneau, the introverted soft-spoken professor of mathematics, has a favorite porn star, and her name is Betlinde. That's it. Just one word. She has dark golden blonde hair and deep dark eyes that complement her tanned skin. She looks formidable and reminds me of a Norse Valkyrie minus the spear and helmet. Any video I can find with Betlinde makes me wet as soon as she appears on the screen. And tonight is no exception. She has on tight black jeans and black boots. Her unfastened leather biker vest does nothing to hide her ample breasts. Her nipples are already erect, and I lick my lips in anticipation of the scene to come. Betlinde has sexy curves, but the best parts of her are that devilish smile and that one raised eyebrow that makes me want to kneel at her feet and do whatever she tells me to do. I always imagine that I am that other woman in the video, that I am the one tied to the bedposts. Betlinde is in charge, you see. I'm thirty-two, single, and more than ready *not* to be in charge of anything.

I've already double checked the blinds and the curtains of my third-floor apartment. They're securely closed against prying eyes. My apartment looks out onto a stand of woods in the back. The leaves are past their peak now that it's mid-November, but the colors outside my window in October were incredible.

Leaves? Seriously? My mind wants to focus on other things right now. Like the fact that there is no direct line of sight from any other apartment. I still have to be careful, though. I can't compromise my position at the university. I have two households to maintain, and it doesn't help that Jen is over two weeks late on her rent payment for the house. Again. Doesn't she know that I still have the mortgage to pay on it? Whatever. Why am I thinking about Jen? She's not here, and Betlinde is.

I hit play on the video and settle into my desk chair. Sometimes I stroke myself in bed and then fall right to sleep afterward, but tonight my toys are spread out on my desk within easy reach. I also like the bigger desktop screen instead of the small screen of my tablet. Once I got over my fear of having sex toys mailed to me, the buying began. There's my current favorite - the clear silicone double-ender. Lately, that's all I want. Penetration. I don't have the double-ender because I anticipate a partner on the other end. No, it just gives me something meaty to grab onto while I penetrate myself.

I sigh. Yep, I'm single again, but there's no use going there in my head. I'm seven months out of my breakup with Jen, and I don't yet remember how to get back out there. And, besides, Betlinde is waiting for me. The scene on the screen is progressing nicely. Betlinde already has the pretty brunette naked and flat on her back on the bed. I suck air through my teeth as Betlinde clamps one hand over the girl's mouth and fastens the girl's left wrist to the bedpost with the other. A surge of pure lust runs through me as I watch her secure the right wrist. The towel I'm sitting on is well on its way to getting soaked.

My right hand journeys south to rake through my wetness. I watch Betlinde feed her right breast into the bound girl's mouth, and I moan along with Betlinde. I lick the middle finger of my left hand and then gently tease each of my nipples in turn with it. God, how I wished I was the girl on the screen, sucking Betlinde's breasts.

"Good girl," Betlinde says to me - I mean to the girl on the screen, but I melt anyway as if she's said it to me. She reaches down, kisses the girl gently on the forehead, and then shimmies up the girl's body, placing her pussy directly over the girl's mouth. "Do what you were born to do, toy."

I moan. I can't help it. I want that to be *my* tongue on her sex. God, I haven't gone down on a woman since forever. Since before Jen. She'd never let me, and I never understood why.

Grr. Why does Jen keeping interrupting my Betlinde time? I pause the video to breathe. In through the nose and out through the mouth. Somewhat focused, I hit play again. An instant surge spikes directly to my clit as the girl runs the flat of her tongue through Betlinde's wetness. My fingers part my pussy lips, and I run three fingers through my slickness, mimicking the girl's tongue.

"Yes, toy," Betlinde says with a moan. "Good, good girl. She's learned her lessons well."

I moan as I watch the girl show Betlinde precisely what she's learned. If I were creating this scene in my head, Betlinde would be inserting her strap-on dildo into me right now. But in my four months of solitude, I've learned to go with the flow and let Betlinde set the pace.

Betlinde moans as she climaxes into the girl's mouth, and it isn't long before my silent plea for Betlinde's strap-on is granted.

Betlinde lithely moves off the girl and leans down close. "Do you want me to fuck you, toy?" Betlinde whispers in her ear.

"Yes. Oh, yes," the girl answers breathlessly.

She receives a sharp slap on her bare breast. The surprise of it makes me jump. Betlinde's left eyebrow raises to the sky. "Yes, *what*, toy?"

The girl grimaces as she says, "Yes, *Mistress*. Yes, please fuck me, *Mistress*."

"Yes, Mistress," I echo. "Please, fuck me." God, how I wish Betlinde were here in the flesh on the other end of that dildo I am about to slide into my wetness.

Betlinde yanks the girl's legs apart. Wide. I lean back in my executive chair and put my feet up on the desk. I slide my feet apart, opening my legs for her. Betlinde runs her fingers through the girl's pussy and then holds them up as if gauging the wetness level. "You're an excited little toy, aren't you?"

"Yes, Mistress," the girl answers. She moans and adds, "You make me hot."

Me, too, I agree in my mind. Betlinde reaches up and puts her fingers in the girl's mouth. I put my fingers in my mouth and lick them clean, just like the girl is doing in the video. I've done this before during my four months of emancipation, and I am surprised every time at how good I taste. I don't know why Jen was so Puritan about oral sex.

Grr, again. Stay the fuck out of my head, Jen.

On the screen, Betlinde takes off her leather vest revealing smooth curvy breasts and strong shoulders. She pulls off her black boots, and I suddenly want to lick and suck her toes. OMG, do I have a foot fetish? Who knew? Betlinde unzips her black jeans, and the tip of a purple dildo peeks out the top. I reach for my clear dildo, getting ready. Wait, she's not wearing a harness. Holy shit, she has on one of those strapless dildos, the kind that is inserted deep into the vagina to keep it in place.

In one swift move, Betlinde yanks the girl's ass to the edge of the bed and plunges into her. I do the same with my clear dildo and cry out at the force of it. Betlinde grips the girl by the hips and pulls out slowly, only to plunge back in quickly. I do the same, and it isn't long before I'm matching Betlinde stroke for stroke. It's like she's fucking me, and I am in heaven.

"Take it like the toy you are," Betlinde says, not missing a stroke.

"Yes, Mistress," I say back to her and moan.

"You're mine."

"Yes, Mistress," I say again. "Yours."

"You're my toy to do with whatever I want," Betlinde says. Her words cause my core to clench. A shudder runs through my body.

I am currently beyond words now and can only moan in reply. Betlinde picks up the pace, and so do I. I lean back further in the chair, the front wheels off the carpet. Teetering backward, I feel the beginnings of my release. I am so close that I have to close my eyes. I only hear Betlinde's voice urging me to hold back my orgasm, that I'd better not cum until she tells me to. My moans of frustration echo the girl's moans on the screen. I'm whimpering in my need at this point.

"Let me cum, Mistress," I growl. My orgasm is right there, teetering on a knife's edge. One pinch of my nipple, and I'll be gone. One flick of my clit will push me over. "Cum now, toy. Cum for me," Betlinde urges me.

I grab one nipple and squeeze hard. The shock of pain goes right to my clit and is just enough to send me over the precipice. I open my throat wide and scream my release as the first wave hits me from somewhere deep inside. I continue to pump the dildo as wave after wave follows. I have never had orgasms this good before. Not with Jen. Not ever.

The clenching pulses inside me slow down. I stop fucking myself just as Betlinde says, "That's my good girl. She likes to be fucked by her Mistress." Betlinde's cooing washes over me, and I am transported further into outer space. My eyes remained glued shut, and I hear Betlinde gently command the girl to lick her clean. The girl must be licking her own juices off Betlinde's purple dildo right about now.

I'll soon do the same, but right now, I am floating free, cradled in Betlinde's arms. I feel, I don't know, like, high or something. My drug is a porn star named Betlinde. I must find out if she has a fan club. Sign up, I will. I smile at my Yoda-ism. My brain goes weird places when I'm floating like this. I ease the dildo out of my pussy and wince. The pounding Betlinde gave me has made me sore. Once my breathing is somewhat under control, I open my eyes and see that the next video is queued up to play. The title reads *Domme Plays with Her submissive*. Betlinde's not in it, and I almost close the window without saving it, but something tells me to bookmark it for another time.

The words *Domme* and *submissive* in the title captivate me. I don't know how I know, but the word *Domme* means female dominant. It might be French, but I'm not sure. And what is weird is that the word *submissive* is not capitalized. And it's part of the title. The nerd part of me is curious, and I need to research further. I gently close my legs and pull my feet off the desk. My pussy lips slide against each other in a puddling mess. Hopefully, I haven't soaked through the towel I'm sitting on. I like this chair; I'd hate to ruin it.

I type the words "Domme and submissive" into my browser's search engine. A myriad of sites, mostly porn, flood my screen. But some sites seem educational, like this one called *BDSMexplained.com*. There are definitions galore. I read what the letters in the acronym BDSM stood for. Bondage & discipline, dominance & submission, sadism & masochism. I've heard of S&M before and know it's not for me. Right? Because S&M is for weirdos. And I'm not a weirdo, am I? But now that I think of it, Betlinde clearly dominated the brunette on the bed. The brunette was submissive to her. And there was bondage in the video, too. My eyes get wider. Betlinde smacked the girl on the breast for not using her proper title. She disciplined the girl. And all of that turned me on.

I sit back in my chair and rub my hands up and down my arms. I am getting cold and should get up to shower and then go to bed. But I don't move. I can't. I am rooted to the chair, wondering why that video turned me on so much. Why did Betlinde's dominance affect me so much?

Bravely, I read on, and the website explains that BDSM is about trust and consent. Did the brunette in the video give Betlinde consent to smack her breast that way? That is puzzling. It also says that a submissive gives power over to the Dominant. Is that what I want? To give someone else power over me. The concept confuses me greatly.

I lean forward and bookmark the website and then type in the phrase, "Am I submissive?" I bookmark several enticing websites to look at later, but one article stands out. "Submission: The New Fad?"

Fad? I, personally, have never heard of dominants and submissives until tonight, so how can this be a fad? The website is called *Kinks.com*. I click on the link, which takes me to a home screen. "*Kinks.com* is a social networking site for those of us with a kinky bent. Over 8-million members strong."

I'm not big on social networking; plastering your life on the Internet for all to see never made much sense to me. But eight million people? Maybe this submission stuff is just a fad. But I don't know anything about it. I need to read this article.

But I can't. You have to be a member. I hesitate for several long minutes, and then curiosity gets the better of me, and I click the button to create a new account. The second it wants a credit card, I'm out. Damn. It wants an email address. I can't use either of my real email addresses, especially not the university-issued addy, and I'm about to give up on the website when a thought comes to me. I could create a fake email address. I could, like, create an alternate personality or something. A quick visit to the Google mail website, and I'm good to go, fake email in hand.

I enter some fake profile information at *Kinks.com* and press enter. I'm in. I can't believe it was that easy. For a while, I tool around the site, appalled at the number of erect penis pictures I see. My eyes sufficiently sift through the dicks, and I finally find the article about submission being a fad. It's not an article, but more of a journal piece. Some guy is writing about his life as a submissive. Oh, my God. I had no idea you could stuff a penis into a tiny cage like that. I had no idea anyone would *want* their penis stuffed into a cage.

I back out of his profile and click around the *Kinks.com* website. My eyes light up when I spot a link to a page for Dommes seeking females submissives. I hold my breath and click the link. Whoa. It's, like, a personals page for Dominant women seeking submissive women for online play or IRL play. What does IRL stand for, I wonder? A quick internet definition tells me that IRL stands for "In Real Life." More clicking reveals that a lot of relationships are online only.

"Hmm," I say out loud to no one. "Online could work." But I'm not quite ready for that step. I have to figure out what this Domme/submissive stuff is all about. I tool around the website for a good hour or more, and by then, I'm ready to fill out my public profile. I can't post an actual picture of my face, but in my opinion, I have nice breasts, so I take a selfie of them up close.

"Betlinde would like these," I say as I admire the picture on my phone. I deem that my breasts will hold up to the million other breasts on *Kinks* and post it. I enter "lesbian" as my orientation and "Antarctica" as my country of origin. Apparently, many people on *Kinks* live there, so I might as well live there, too. I can't have my students or colleagues putting the pieces together and finding out that I am "crystal_toy." I reason that a torso only picture makes me fit in with the rest of the women on *Kinks*. They don't see my short boyish haircut and the fact that I'm a soft butch. Perusing the various members' pages, I don't see anyone that looks like me. But what else is new? Most of my lesbian friends are femme in one way or another. Me? I'm strictly no makeup, no women's clothes except bras. I do wear women's underwear, but fittingly they're called boi shorts.

As I meander around people's profiles and writings, I discover that the lowercase *s* in the word submissive is symbolic and indicates that submissives are below Dominants with their capital *D*. It's a tidy system that makes perfect sense to me. The most challenging section to fill in is that D/s status. Who am I? *What* am I? I scan the list and don't think I'm a sadist or a masochist. And I'm not even sure what *pets* or *littles* are. And if I don't know what they are, I can't possibly be one. Seriously? I don't think I could pull off the Betlinde role, so a Dominant I am not. But I desperately want to be underneath her, so I decide that submissive is best for me. The profile also wants me to list what I'm looking for.

"Good question," I say to the screen as I look over the choices. I pick two. I let the kinky people at *Kinks.com* know that I am looking for either a play partner or a Mistress.

A glance at the clock tells me it's getting late, and I have to get ready for my early Calculus 1 class. I peel myself off the chair and head to the kitchen to set up the coffee pot for the morning and then make a bag lunch. I've been brown-bagging it for four months ever since money got tight supporting the two households. I chuckle when I catch my naked reflection in the refrigerator. It's weird walking around the apartment without clothes on, but I kind of like the freedom of it.

I go back to my computer to bookmark the *Kinks* page, and I am about to shut down the computer for the night when my hand freezes on the mouse. There is a little red number one on top of the mail icon. I have mail. It's from someone named Mistress_Ciara. Oh, fuck. What have I done?

Chapter Two

How Wet Are You?

With eyes wide, I carefully power down my computer without opening the *Kinks* message from Mistress_Ciara. What the hell have I gotten myself into? And, besides, how freaking needy and eager would it seem if I answered her tonight? I'm zonked from my release with Betlinde, anyway, and it's a school night, too. These are just excuses, I know, but I'm scared to death. And that message will still be there in the morning. Won't it?

I'm a tiny bit freaked out about what I just did—signing up for a kinky sex site? Really? I scurry to the shower as if to wash off my shame and then dive into bed. I slam my eyes shut. Did I just make a huge mistake? I go over it again and again. My real name and location are nowhere on that website, right? Mistress_Ciara has no idea I live in Cincinnati. Right? *Stop worrying*, I tell myself without conviction. And then I retrace my steps again and again until I finally fall asleep from mental exhaustion.

Upon rising the next morning, I don't dare power on my laptop. What if there are seven hundred messages from other Mistresses or something?

"That's a little presumptuous," I say out loud as I pour coffee into my commuter mug. "My tits aren't that amazing." I laugh and vow to put *Kinks.com* and Dommes and submissives into the back of my mind. I grab my briefcase, toss my bag lunch inside, and head out the door.

The forty-minute drive gives me plenty of time to think. But not about Dommes. Nope, I have an eight a.m. Calculus 1 class to think about. The Mathematics Department needs someone to teach these lower-level courses, and it's been me every year for five years. I guess I have the patience for freshmen. But what I really want to teach are the 400-level and higher courses. I'd love to dig into some abstract algebra. My dissertation covered aspects of group theory and commutative rings.

"Bah," I say out loud and unlock the door to my office. There's no sense getting excited about a branch of mathematics I can't dig into right now. Research is secondary to teaching at the university. That's what attracted me to it in the first place. That's why I left California to come here to Ohio. But still. There's that Johnson article about Sylow Theorems I've been dying to devour, but whatever. My time will come.

After my fifty-minute lecture, I sit in my closet of an office waiting for any wayward freshmen to darken my door. As if. It doesn't matter if they come or not. I faithfully sit for office hours, unlike my colleagues who seem to think office hours are optional. I have a stack of problem sets I could be grading, but I simply cannot focus. My mind keeps marching back to Betlinde and *Kinks.com* and Mistress_Ciara. I wish I had a graduate assistant to help me with this grading, so I can just go home. Everyone else seems to have one, except me. Dr. Wainwright, the department chair, told me there wasn't enough in the budget when I requested one. I need to find a way to insist. My courses have the largest enrollment, so why shouldn't I get the help I need? I vow to put in for a graduate assistant for the spring semester.

When my office hours are officially over, I spend another couple of hours fine-tuning tomorrow's Elementary Functions class for non-math majors who need math credits to graduate. I also catch up on a few emails. Now it's finally time for lunch. I typically eat in the small break room behind the copy machine with the administrative assistants and non-teaching staff. I call them the ladies who lunch. All the ladies in there seem to dote on me like the moms that they are. They were a tremendous collective support during my breakup with Jen. But today I am antsy and decide to go home. Thoughts of Mistress_Ciara's message have me ill-equipped to focus on much of anything else. And, besides, no one will miss me, I'm sure about that. But if someone does, I can always say I wasn't feeling well. I am feeling kind of dizzy, but not too dizzy to realize I should stop by the house and see if Jen has a rent check for me. But why should I? She signed a lease and knows when her rent is due. I follow the rules. Why can't she?

I feel a mixture of relief and dread as I enter my apartment. I'm relieved that now the world can't read my face and know that I am a sexual deviant who's joined a kinky website, and I dread that I've done just that. I throw my bag lunch into the fridge; I'll take that to school tomorrow. I change into sweats and a t-shirt and heat some leftovers. The computer is sitting there so innocently, taunting me. There is only one thing that can help me right now, and that is wine—leftover wine to go with leftover lunch.

Glass in hand, I sit in my desk chair and power up the computer. I type *Kinks.com* in my browser. My home page pops up right where I left it. I squint because I am afraid of what I will see. Oh, crap, the mailbox number is no longer a one. It is now a crooked number. Four. I have four messages. Oh, God, do I have to answer each one? My mother, God rest her soul, taught me to be polite. Would it be rude to read the messages and delete them? Will those people *know* that I deleted their messages without responding? What if I don't even read them? Will they know that, too?

"What's that?" I say to the wine glass. "Let's avoid the mail for now. Sounds good. Let's perv away on other people's pages."

I spend a good half-hour looking at the amazing bodies. It's incredible how much skin and body parts people post publicly. I realize that each picture has a button you can click to "like" it. I am about to press the "like" button for one particularly curvy black woman's breasts and torso when I stop mid-click. Can others see what I'm doing? Will this woman know that it was me who "liked" her photo? Upon further inspection, I realize that not only will she know, but the entire populace of *Kinks* will know, too. I carefully move my mouse away from the like button and unclick.

I sigh and wonder why I am such scared. My gaze takes me up to the top of my monitor, and I notice the little camera there. Oh, shit. I've heard stories about people remotely accessing your computer and watching you. I slam the screen down on my laptop. I touched myself in front of that screen yesterday. Oh. My. God. I stand up and head to the kitchen to get more wine and something to cover the camera. One more glass of wine and one post-it-note securely taped over the camera later, and I am back on *Kinks*.

All those pictures of beautiful bodies have me kind of worked up. My favorite pics seem to be the ones of female torsos, especially those with a nice set of curvy boobs. I check the blinds and the curtains. Yep, they are still armored shut from last night. Feeling sexy, I strip bare, including my socks, and sit down on a fresh towel. The cool air feels refreshing on my exposed skin.

"You've stalled long enough, chicken," I scold myself out loud. I take a full minute to breathe and gather my courage. A few sips of the wine give me that bravery I need. I click the mail icon, and the four separate messages pop up. A glance shows that three are from guys. I can tell by the three dicks in my inbox. Didn't I make it clear on my home page that I am a lesbian and not interested in guys? I guess they don't care, do they? Maybe they each think they can be *the one* to finally convert me, that their dick is *the* dick of all dicks, and I obviously don't know what I've been missing. No, I will not suck your dick. No, I do not want your dick up my ass. What was that last one? Oh, yeah, no, I do not want you to tie me up and whip me. Three quick delete clicks later, and I'm left stating at the one remaining message.

I take a deep breath and then click the icon. Mistress_Ciara's message opens on my screen.

> MISTRESS_CIARA: Hello, crystal_toy. your profile picture is gorgeous. your breasts are full and firm. Those nipples look so inviting. I want to lean closer, lick

My lips, and then gently secure clamps to them. How tight shall I secure them, crystal-toy?

MISTRESS_CIARA: I would love to see more of that beautiful body of yours. I would love to feel your lips caress My own nipples, making them peak in excitement as you take them into your mouth one at a time. your tongue will make them hard, which lets you know that you please your Mistress. I'll pull your head tighter against My chest as a signal for you to suck until I'm so aroused that I put both hands on the top of your head and push you down to your knees. I'll part my legs slightly in invitation.

MISTRESS_CIARA: You know what to do now, don't you, crystal-toy? your tongue will be on My clit within seconds, licking and sucking My flesh just the way I like it, because every good slave knows how to please her Mistress, doesn't she?

MISTRESS_CIARA: After I cum all over your lips, you'll lick Me clean. And then I'll pull you down on all fours by the collar and leash I've attached around your neck; the collar and leash that means you are My property. Would you like this, crystal-toy? Are you wet? How wet are you? Message Me and tell Me how much you want Me to move behind you and grab you firmly by the hips and slowly tease open your dripping cunt with the tip of My BBC.

MISTRESS_CIARA: Tell Me, crystal-toy, tell Me how much you want Me to push deep inside you.

A surge of pure adrenaline spikes through my core. "Oh. My. God," I eke out, half moaning. "You don't even know how fucking wet you've made me," I say to her words. I moan again. I am so turned on. I'm breathing hard. They're just words on a screen, but I reread them from the beginning, and another surge of adrenaline rushes through me. I have no idea what a BBC is, but whatever it is, she has permission to fuck me with it. Oh, God, if only this woman were really here doing those things to me. I take a deep breath and blow out a long sigh. I should be appalled that anyone dared speak to me the way she did in her message. I was offended by the sexual messages I got from those guys, but Mistress_Ciara is a woman. And I am far from offended.

"Yes, Mistress," I say out loud. "Yes, I want this." I don't even have to check to see how wet I am. I know I am soaking, but I check anyway. I slide my fingers down, and it's just like I thought. I'm as slick as I was last night when Betlinde had her way with me. I pull my fingers out. They are glistening with my tangible excitement. Instead of wiping my fingers on a tissue, I put them in my mouth and imagine I am sucking Mistress_Ciara's fingers.

Reality kicks in when I realize that I don't know anything about Mistress_Ciara. I quickly wipe my fingers on a tissue, grab the mouse, and click on her name. This sends me to her page. I melt. She is beautiful. And she looks strong and Dominant. And she is black. Her skin is so lovely and smooth and dark. Her lips are full and kissable. I try to take in every detail at once, and I end up getting a little dizzy.

"Focus," I say out loud and purposely don't look at the screen for a moment. There is too much information to take in. I reach for my wine and am amazed that the glass is empty. I stand up and walk to the kitchen for more. It's the middle of a Monday afternoon, and I already have a nice buzz going. Did I eat lunch? I can't remember. Yes, there's the empty bowl. My mind is a wasteland right now.

I grab the entire wine bottle out of the fridge and bring it with me to the computer. This will save time because I realize that I plan on answering

Mistress_Ciara's message, which will take a lot of fortitude, the kind I can only get from fermented grapes.

I pour the Zinfandel into my glass and take a sip. I look at her profile picture again. "You're so pretty. So curvy. So sexy." I lean closer and mumble, "Now, where are you from?" My jaw drops open when I see that she is from Columbus. That's so close, less than two hours away from Cincinnati. My heart races. Wait, wait, wait, she doesn't know I'm from Cin-city. Technically, I'm from Antarctica. She'll understand that I can't reveal my true location, won't she? Most of the people on this website have to be careful about their vanilla life. I chuckle at my use of the word *vanilla*. I've only been a member of this website for maybe, like, fifteen hours total, and I already know some of the lingo. But anyway, maybe Mistress_Ciara has to be careful with her vanilla life, too. Maybe not, though. She has a full-face picture on her page, and she listed her city. Maybe she doesn't have to be careful. Or maybe, just maybe, she doesn't really live in Columbus, and maybe that picture of her isn't really her, and maybe she's a guy. Oh, shit. What if this whole thing is a setup, and it's just a guy trying to get me to…to what?

"To do *things*!" I answer out loud. Isn't it obvious? Oh, great, now I'm not only talking to myself, but I'm arguing. Yeesh. I turn to the half-empty glass of wine sitting on the cardboard coaster and ask it a serious question, "What do you think?" I nod in agreement. "More exploration is needed. I concur."

Cool. She, or he, is forty. That's eight years older than I am. Maybe that means she or he is experienced. Okay, this 'she or he' bullshit is tiring already. I am just going to believe Mistress_Ciara is a woman or at least woman-identified. What if she's a transgender male to female? Hmm, I never thought about a transgender partner before. As long as she is woman-identified, then, yeah, I'd go for it, for the right person.

"All right," I say to the universe, "Mistress_Ciara is officially a woman until I hear differently."

That settled, I click on the link to her pictures. Oh, my God. She isn't shy about showing her skin, now is she? I perv around her collection of photos. Her breasts are large with dark chocolate chip nipples, and she has a curvy figure, which she doesn't seem to mind showing to everyone. Oh, God, look at her ass. I want to run my hands over her soft flesh. So round and luscious.

I laugh. "Really, Bernadette?" I say out loud. "Did you just think the word *luscious*?" *Why, yes. Yes, I did.* And it's true. This woman is incredible. Almost too good to be true.

"What are you into, *luscious* Mistress_Ciara?" I click back to her main page. She has a list of fetishes. She is into receiving "pussy worship." Check. I can do that. She is also into "dominating women." Maybe I wouldn't mind being dominated? I don't know. All I have to go on is Betlinde, and I sure wouldn't mind her dominating me.

"Oh, God, you're into giving anal penetration," I say to her online picture. "I don't know about that one, Miss Missy Mistress_Ciara." I've never done anything like that. I never thought to ask Jen to explore this with me. I guess I was afraid of getting something stuck and then having to explain to the emergency room staff why a professor of mathematics had something lodged up her ass. No, thank you. A lot of people on *Kinks* have a list of things they are *not* into and won't do. These, I learned, are called hard limits.

"Is anal one of my hard limits?" My eyes get wide. I have no idea. But I definitely know that I am not into piss or scat play and can't believe that anyone is. "Don't judge," I scold myself. I remember reading something on someone else's *Kinks* page. "Your kink may not be my kink, but I defend your right to express it."

"Keep an open mind, Dr. Garneau," I say to myself. "You're new to all of this." I nod in agreement.

Neither of my two hard limits, it seems, are fetishes of hers, thank God. My eyes widen as I read her list of things she likes to give. They include *leash and collar training, orgasm denial, double penetration, spanking, 'you belong to Me' whispered in her ear, CNC.*

"What the hell is *CNC*?" I wonder out loud. "They sure like acronyms on this website. I have to look up *BBC*, too. Should I make a list?" No, someone might see it.

And then I burst out laughing. "Who the fuck comes into your apartment, idiot? You have no one. Jordan's in San Francisco. He and Cathy take care of Dad full time, and Mom died right before I moved out to Cincinnati. A year before I met Jen. And now you don't even have Jen or any friends because Jen took them all, even the ones you had *before* she showed up."

I stand up abruptly, angry for allowing those stuffed down, lonely, woe-is-me feelings to surface. I stomp to the bathroom and relieve my bladder and then stomp right back to my chair in the living room. My mood softens a little when I realize how much easier going to the bathroom is when you have no clothes on.

"Okay, Mistress_Ciara," I say, determined to throw a small bit of caution to the wind. "Here goes."

I hit the reply button and start typing whatever comes out of my fingertips.

CRYSTAL_TOY: Mistress_Ciara, your message was a delightful surprise. Thank you. I am newly discovering my submissive side and am brand spanking (pun intended) new.

CRYSTAL_TOY: I would love to chat further with you and see where it goes. I am intrigued not only by your words but by your pictures, too. You are a beautiful woman. And I enjoyed reading your fetish list, too. Everything there seems so intriguing.

I've never written erotica before, but there's always a first time, so here goes.

CRYSTAL_TOY: Your hands on the back of my head pull me to your breast, and I suck your nipple hard and then lightly bite the flesh surrounding it as my tongue gives your sensitive flesh a good tongue-lashing. You moan at my ministrations, and you move me to the other nipple. I want to stay here for a while and become one with your breasts, but you have other ideas, don't you?

CRYSTAL_TOY: Your hands push me lower. I know what that means. Mistress is pleased with me and is going to reward me with time at her altar. The pressure on my head is slight, and I know this means I am to worship your body as I travel lower. I am turned on by the darkness of your skin, Mistress. The contrast between your dark skin and my white is intoxicating. As is your scent. I inhale your earthy muskiness and allow myself a moment to breathe you in. You part your legs. This is my signal to make direct contact. I kiss your outer lips and gently suck them into my mouth. I then lick your swollen pussy from back to front. I ignore your clit. No, actually, I'm not ignoring it. I'm saving it for last. Savoring it.

CRYSTAL_TOY: You have other ideas, though, and smash my face against it. 'Please me,' is all you say. I press the flat of my tongue against your nub and then lick you until the tip of my tongue slowly encircles you. I latch my lips around you and suck gently. You grab my face and keep me still. You like this. This is my signal to flick my tongue and make you cum all over my face. I hold on as best I can while you buck and rub against my face. I love making you cum, Mistress. It is a privilege. Will you teach me other ways to please you, Mistress? If it pleases you to fuck me with your BBC …

I pause for a minute and open a new tab on my browser to hit up *UrbanDictionary.com* for a BBC definition. "Oh," I say, wide-eyed. "Big Black Cock. Okay, then." I should look up CNC, too, but I want to finish my message to her before running out of courage.

My fingers hover over the keyboard. I groan and hide my face behind both hands. What am I doing? Asking an invisible stranger to fuck me? Holy shit. "You've lost it, Bernadette," I say out loud.

I take a moment, still hiding my face behind my hands, and then final peek out from behind them. I reread what I've already written, and my entire body clenches with sexual energy. "Fuck it," I say to no one. My hands go back to the keyboard and finish my sentence.

> CRYSTAL_TOY: … then, yes, Mistress, do it. I am wet for you, Mistress. I'm spreading my legs wide.

I find myself doing that in my chair as I type the words. I can't help it. I am so turned on.

> CRYSTAL_TOY: Pull me down by my leash onto all fours. How wet am I, you asked? So wet that you can slide your BBC into my tight pussy with one swift thrust. Please, take me hard, Mistress.

A sigh forces itself out of me. "Mmm," I moan again. I close my eyes and picture her behind me, pushing in and out. Her black hands grab my hips for leverage. She pulls me to her as she slams into me over and over.

> CRYSTAL_TOY: Mistress, I'm ready to cum. Please, let me cum, Mistress. I will cum hard for you. I will scream your name when my pussy clenches around your thrusting BBC. Mistress, will you let me cum?

I am so fucking horny right now, but I don't dare touch myself or even squeeze my legs together. I need to stay focused and reread my reply message. I can't believe I'm going to send a message like this to a stranger. Oh. My. God.

Who knows? I may never hear from her again. Satisfied with my reply, I steel myself and hit the send button. Afterward, I hold my breath for a moment. Oh, God, what did I just do?

"You volleyed it right back to her, Bernadette. That's what you did." I grin. *Yep*, I thought. *I sent a wine-fueled volley right back to Columbus-frickin' Ohio.* "Let's see what you do with that, Mistress." I stand up in search of another bottle of wine.

Chapter Three

Mistress Ciara

The new bottle of wine is open and sitting ready on my desk. My glass is filled. I am back in my command chair, squirming. Mistress_Ciara's message and my suggestive response has me more turned on than I've ever been. This is real. The towel underneath me is damp, but I don't care. That's why the building has a washer and dryer in the basement. I wonder if Mistress_Ciara is still at work or if she works from home. Has she seen my reply yet? It would take her a few minutes to read it, so I resist the urge to look at the mailbox icon.

Oh, shit. She'll probably check out my page the same way I checked out hers. I quickly edit my profile and select *No Piss* and *No Scat* as hard limits. I want Mistress_Ciara to see my hard limits displayed upfront in black and white, just so there is no misunderstanding. Do I have more hard limits? I think back on all the profiles I've read. Yes, humiliation. I don't want that. Men. I don't want that either and add those to my hard limits. Since she seems to love anal so much, I put *Anal Training* as something I'm curious about. As far as my fetishes go, I have yet to figure that out. I perv around other people's pages and find a few that will work for now. I get five more fetishes up there, and it's a good start. I am now into receiving *a woman who knows how to take control, lesbian Dommes, orgasm control, teach me I'm still learning*, and *breast play*. I put in the *orgasm control* fetish because Mistress_Ciara has that on her page. Maybe she'll see that and smile and want to play with me.

And what's weird is that even though I am so turned on and horny right now, I haven't reached for any of my dildos. Even my fingers haven't reached to stroke my clit or plunge inside me. I could cum so quickly right now. Why haven't I touched myself? I give that question pause. Am I waiting for permission from her? A stranger on the Internet? That's absurd.

I tagged myself as "submissive" on the *Kinks* website, but I'm not exactly sure what that means, though. After meandering through the site and reading people's posts and writings, I understand that submission can happen in the bedroom only, or it can happen 24/7. As an independent woman, how can I even think about letting someone control me every hour of the day and every day of every week? This is what some of those conservative men believe women should do. No way. I'm a feminist. I will *not* let someone control me just because I am a woman.

"But you'd be giving yourself to another *woman*," I muse out loud. That one stumps me.

And what about the bedroom? Can I submit there? I have always played the role of the top in every sexual relationship I've ever had. And I've always hated it. Because I look and dress like a butch, all of my partners expected me to be the aggressor. And if I hadn't taken charge, nothing would have happened in most of those relationships.

But being submissive in the bedroom? If it's anything like being under Betlinde's dominance, then yes, I can be submissive in the bedroom. That's a sure-fire thing. Maybe that's why I haven't touched myself. Maybe I've already given Mistress_Ciara control of my orgasms. Another wave of lust runs through me at the thought. Am I submitting to her already?

I sip on my wine, but my stomach protests a little. Shit. This second bottle is already half empty. I tap the cork back in and get up to put it in the fridge. I've had enough for now. I need to be level-headed if she responds. And, besides, I'm feeling just the right kind of fine at the moment, except that I have to pee again.

24

I barely remember peeing because my head is filled with questions. Was I submissive to Jen without realizing it? Did I kowtow to every one of Jen's commands? Yes, usually, but that was to keep the peace and avoid the inevitable fight. When I gave in to her like that, was that submission?

I head back to my command chair, thinking about my ex. She still lives in my house. "*My* fucking house," I say out loud and stab the air with my finger. "Why do *I* have to live in this shitty third-floor walkup apartment? How the fuck did I let that happen?"

I sigh and look down at my bare feet. I should clip my toenails.

"And you're avoiding the question, asswipe," I growl at myself. "All right. All right." I put my hands up defensively. "It was quicker and easier to move out." I didn't want a long drawn out break up. I can't believe the balls I had demanding she sign that lease, though. Thank God for realtors who handle that shit.

Our breakup shocked all of our friends. And they all sided with Jen. Who knows what lies she told them. No one reached out to me or stuck by me. No one. But, then again, I never told anyone *my* side of the story. The side that is the truth. The truth is that Jen and I fell out of love. That we're barely friends now. Whatever. Fuck 'em. Who needs them?

The question I'd asked myself earlier came back to me. Was I submissive to Jen? I walk over to the window and am just about to move the curtain to peek out when I remember that I am naked. Instead, I look at the three photographs hanging on my apartment walls. They are pictures from each of my three college graduations. My family was with me for all three. Mom had passed on from pancreatic cancer right before I got my Ph.D. from UC Berkeley, so it was just Jordan and me and Dad in that picture.

Mom wasn't submissive to Dad. Nor was Dad submissive to her. They had a great partnership. That's what I thought I had with Jen, but after a couple of years – right when the sex dried up – she wanted her way all the time. Was that dominance? Or was she just domineering? It was more like assholery, if you ask me.

I went back to the computer and searched the *Kinks* website about submission and found a group geared toward newbie submissives. Was that me? I officially joined it, and my eyes opened wide when I read that being a submissive does *not* mean you are an underling. You have the right to demand respect and safety from your Dominant. Submissives, apparently, trust their Dominants enough to hand over the reins completely. In a 24/7 relationship, handing over the reins can mean all kinds of things. The basic idea is that the Dominant makes all or most decisions about the household and the relationship and everything.

"How do you *not* become an underling in that scenario? A mere servant?" I ask out loud. "How do you keep yourself intact? It sounds like slavery to me." I read on and chuckle out loud when I find an article comparing and contrasting slavery and submission. It's like they're reading my mind. Maybe all newbies go through this same kind of thought process. The article says that unlike slavery, a submissive has control over some things. They have the right to negotiate aspects of the relationship. And the next two lines blow my mind. "A submissive is equal to her Dominant. The key is power exchange." I sigh. Once I feel as if I understand something, they throw another concept at me. *Power exchange.* What is that?

My stomach growls, and I realize I have been reading about BDSM for hours. I checked the mail icon every few minutes during that time, of course, but it has remained stubbornly dark. It's already five o'clock, and I need some food ASAP. My stomach is majorly sour from the wine. I toss a frozen pizza in the oven and pop open a Coke. I should probably drink some water, but I need the caffeine to wake me up a little. The wine has me wanting to take a nap. And that I cannot do. What if Mistress_Ciara replies to my message and I'm sleeping off an afternoon bender?

I bring my soda and now-heated pizza back to the computer. I look up at the mail icon that I've glanced up at a million times that afternoon. My eyes widen. The icon is no longer dark. A red number one is stamped on top. My mouth goes dry. Is it her? I blow out a nervous sigh and take a couple of bites of pizza. I need strength. I need fortification. I need a lobotomy. What have I gotten myself into, I ask not for the first time.

Relax, relax, relax, I tell myself. It's probably just another fabulous dick pic showing up in my inbox. Blowing out another sigh, I click the mail icon. My adrenaline spikes when I see it *is* from her. Oh, my God, Mistress_Ciara has responded. I click it open. The message is short.

> MISTRESS_CIARA: Good girl. Are you avail for about an hour at seven this evening?

My heart is pounding. What if she wants to Skype or video-chat or see my face? That can't happen. I'll have to find a paper bag. Or a ski mask. I have one, I think. No, dammit, that's still at Jen's. My Cincinnati Bengal's hat pulled down over my face? Maybe. That might work.

> CRYSTAL_TOY: Yes, Mistress. I am available at that time.

Her reply comes back within seconds.

> MISTRESS_CIARA: Did you touch yourself today, crystal_toy? Did you make yourself cum?

I hold my breath as my pussy clenches at her words. I can't believe she's asking me this. And I can't believe I'm responding.

> CRYSTAL_TOY: No. I wanted to. But I didn't.

I add that last part to let her know that she is in charge.

> MISTRESS_CIARA: Those were all the right words, pet. Are you shaved?

I melt, and I am appalled both at once. I melt because she called me "pet." I'm appalled because, Jee-zus, there's nothing like getting personal right away.

CRYSTAL_TOY: No, I'm not shaved.

MISTRESS_CIARA: Looks like you have about an hour and a half to get that done then. Chat with you at seven, pet.

I am stunned. Did I just receive my first command from a Mistress? Do I even want to shave down there? I look down at my patch of pubic hair. I always keep myself trimmed and neat, but shaved? This is going to take some thought.

"The clock is ticking," my brain tells me. "I know. I know. Hush. I'm thinking. I have to respond to her."

I click in the chatting window where my reply goes and type.

CRYSTAL_TOY: Yes, Mistress. I will figure out how to do that. See you at seven.

I wait a few minutes as I munch on my pizza, waiting to see if she replies. It becomes clear that she isn't going to, so I click open a new tab in my browser and hit up *YouTube.com* for a video about shaving, you know, down there. This Mistress will never know if I do it or not because there is no way in hell I'm going to do video chatting. No way.

But then it hits me. She's going to demand proof. She's going to want me to post more pictures or send them to her. Shit, shit, shit. I have to figure out how to do this. I am in shock at the sheer number of videos addressing shaving down below, and it isn't long before I'm in the shower shaving myself smooth using the techniques I learned mere minutes ago.

I must have shaved seven times just to make sure I got everything. I even shaved around my butthole. Who even knew that hair grew back there? Several checks with a handheld mirror confirm that I am now clean-shaven.

I get out of the shower and apply a quick swipe of alcohol with a few cotton balls. It stings like crazy, but one of the videos I watched suggested this step to make sure no bacteria gets in the hair follicles. Apparently, this is to minimize red bumps. After a few minutes, I apply baby oil to the area. I am amazed at how smooth things are down there. It's kind of sexy and is turning me on a little. No, a lot.

Once I am completely shaved, I step out of my comfort zone and prop one foot up on the closed toilet lid and position my phone between my legs. I snap a few pictures making sure no details of my bathroom or the rest of me show. If she wants proof, she'll get it. I snap one last photo of my blue bathroom rug just so my vagina is not the first picture staring out from my camera roll.

I don't bother getting dressed and head back into the living room to figure out what to do while I wait for an agonizingly long forty-five minutes to tick by.

Chapter Four

What Have I Gotten Myself Into?

Even though my stomach keeps protesting, I snarf down my now ice-cold pizza because I know I'll need strength for Mistress_Ciara later. My whole core quivers in anticipation. I need a distraction. And what better distraction is there than grading Calculus problem sets in the nude?

I set a timer for 6:55 pm because I know myself. Once I get immersed in work, I lose all sense of time, and I cannot be late for my first meeting with Mistress_Ciara. I'm only giving myself five minutes to get ready for her. More than that would fray my already frayed nerves.

Grading my students' work is familiar and calms me. I almost, but not quite, get my nerves settled through the process. There has always been something soothing for me about the beauty and preciseness of mathematics. As I work, I analyze my students' issues. Many of them are struggling with the algebra that is essential for solving first-order differential equations. It's not the calculus that's tripping them up but the algebra. I open my planner and make a note to address it for tomorrow's lecture. I jump when my alarm goes off.

"Shit." I put a hand over my spasming heart. I turn off the alarm. "Holy fuck." I take a deep breath and let it out slowly. I take another breath and then get up to hit the bathroom and wash my hands and face. I am about to embark into a strange land with Mistress_Ciara, not even twenty-four hours after declaring my kinkiness on *Kinks.com*.

I make myself a large glass of ice water. No more wine because I need a clear head. I turn on my favorite eighties rock station to cover any prying neighbors' ears. I sit down in my command chair and log in. My message icon is dark. She isn't here yet. I take a sip of water and then pack up the papers I was grading and stuff them in my briefcase, ready for tomorrow. Seven o'clock comes and goes. It is now 7:05, and there is no sign of Mistress_Ciara. I am one part disappointed, and one part relieved. My nerves can't take this waiting, so I stand up to head into the kitchen to set up my coffee pot for tomorrow. Just as I stand, a red number one appears on my message icon.

I lunge for my desk, click on the icon, and throw myself back in the chair. My message box opens. It's from her. It's from her. It's from her. I take a quick breath and open her message.

> MISTRESS_CIARA: It is customary for pets to arrive early and announce their presence.
>
> CRYSTAL_TOY: I'm here.

I'm not sure what to add, so I let my message stand.

> MISTRESS_CIARA: It's obvious that you need training. I will not be kept waiting again. Do you understand this?
>
> CRYSTAL_TOY: Yes, ma'am. Is it okay to call you ma'am? How should I address you?

I'm panicking now. She spotted me as a newbie instantly. Shit. But I *am* a newbie. Maybe she likes newbies. Shut up, I tell myself. Get your shit together.

MISTRESS_CIARA: I'm glad you're concerned about protocols, pet. This is a good thing. I will address that momentarily.

She called me "pet" again. I am melting in my chair while my southern region is getting very warm.

MISTRESS_CIARA: I see that you live in Antarctica, which means you need to be careful with your vanilla life. I understand this and will honor this. I do, however, require My pets to send and/or post pictures. And I will reciprocate by sending you pictures. That is only fair. Will this be a problem?

Oh, God. Here it is right up front. I swallow down my anxiety and type in something that I'm not sure is the truth.

CRYSTAL_TOY: No problem on my end. I am, however, somewhat of a public figure and cannot have my face or name or location disclosed.

Okay, that public figure thing is a stretch, but then again, it's not. I teach a lot of students. At this point in my career, they number in the thousands. Being outed like this would not go well for me career-wise or reputation-wise.

MISTRESS_CIARA: I understand. W/we can work out specific details later. I'll give you My private email in a bit. One thing W/we need to work on immediately is how you address Me. you may refer to Me as Mistress, Mistress Ciara, or Ma'am. you will capitalize these. Do you understand?

CRYSTAL_TOY: Yes, I do.

MISTRESS_CIARA: Yes, I do, *what*?

Shit. What does she want? I am at a loss. I can feel the artery in my neck throbbing as my heart surges with adrenaline. I read back over her last few lines. Then it dawns on me.

CRYSTAL_TOY: Yes, I do, *Mistress*.

MISTRESS_CIARA: Good girl. you are intelligent and catch on quickly. I like that.

I breathe out a sigh of relief. I passed my first test.

MISTRESS_CIARA: Another item of protocol is for you to remember *your* place. Always keep yourself lower than Me. Sit at My feet or sit in a chair that is lower than Mine. you walk at least one step behind Me. Always.

MISTRESS_CIARA: Also, refer to yourself in lowercase letters. i, i'm, me, my. Always lowercase, even at the start of a sentence. It is your way of acknowledging that I am your Dominant. Is this understood, pet?

CRYSTAL_TOY: Yes, i understand, Mistress.

I check over the sentence three times before I hit enter.

MISTRESS_CIARA: Good. you please Me.

I don't know why, but my southland flutters wildly at her praise.

> MISTRESS_CIARA: I see your white skin in your online picture, pet. As I told you earlier, I expect all of My white girls to be clean-shaven. Did you take care of this?

All? *All* of her white girls? How many does she have? Does she have any black girls? Asian girls? Indigenous peoples? I feel momentarily insulted that I am not her only girl. Who is this person in Columbus, Ohio that sees me as just one more plaything in her corral? I laugh when I see my *Kinks.com* name on the computer screen: crystal_toy. I made it clear that I was to be someone's toy, someone's plaything, just by the name I chose. I am reaping what I have sowed.

I get over my momentary disappointment and go back to her request. The request that I knew was coming. She wants proof that I followed her first official command.

> CRYSTAL_TOY: Yes, Mistress, i took care of it. i am now clean-shaven. It feels freeing, actually.

I add the last part to give her a little bit of my personality.

> MISTRESS_CIARA: I will need proof, pet. *Kinks.com* doesn't allow for picture exchanges in their message service. you can post your pic on *Kinks* for 'friends only' viewing, or you can send the pic to My private email: CiaraOwnsyou@gmail.com. And I will want this proof soon – before our time together is finished tonight.

CRYSTAL_TOY: Yes, Ma'am. My private email is Crystal562@gmail.com. I will send a picture presently.

I cringe and pull my hand away from the keyboard as I see that I forgot to lowercase the words 'my' and 'i'. I fix it hastily and then hit send. Shit, I almost messed up within the first ten minutes of conversing with a Dominant.

MISTRESS_CIARA: you anticipated My request, didn't you?

CRYSTAL_TOY: Yes, Mistress.

I hit the Gmail app on my phone and make triply sure I am on my new fake email screen and save her email information to my contacts list. She is the first and only contact Crystal562 has. With a deep breath, I click on the 'compose new email' icon. I upload the best picture of my newly shorn pussy and then type in her email address in the To: section. I close my eyes and blow out a sigh. This is becoming really real at this point. I don't care. I hit send.

Within seconds Mistress Ciara replies.

MISTRESS_CIARA: you have a stunning white-girl cunt. So pink and luscious. Thank you for sending it. you are beautiful, pet.

My southern tier creams at her words. I can't believe how wet she is making me.

My phone chimes at an incoming email. It's from her. I open it, and in my inbox is a picture of her 'inbox'. She sent me a close-up of her beautiful pussy. I stare like a teenage boy at my prize. My mouth hangs open. Her black skin accentuates the gorgeous pinkness of her inner folds.

The color contrast is outstanding. I tell her so and thank her for sending me a part of herself.

My words seem to stroke her ego.

MISTRESS_CIARA: Now you may worship your Mistress, even when W/we are apart.

She has a bit of an ego, I realize. But then again, Dominants have to be confident people, don't they? Yeah, I could never be a Dominant.

MISTRESS_CIARA: pet?

CRYSTAL_TOY: Yes, Mistress?

MISTRESS_CIARA: What are you wearing?

I moan as a spike of pure lust zips through my body at her question.

CRYSTAL_TOY: Umm...i am wearing my birthday suit.

MISTRESS_CIARA: LOL. Good girl. Are you wet, pet?

CRYSTAL_TOY: Very.

MISTRESS_CIARA: Let me verify this. I dip my fingers through your folds and plunge them deep into your cunt.

While I imagine her fingers doing just that, I realize that maybe I'm supposed to mimic her movements. I don't want to ask if I can touch myself because it might break the mood, so I just do it. I slide my fingers over my smoothly shaved mons and shiver. The smoothness is so sexy. Why didn't I do this years ago? My fingers find my slick folds and push inside. Deep, she said, so I push as far as they will reach.

MISTRESS_CIARA: Yes, you are wet, My pet. Take My fingers. Put them in your mouth. Clean them for Me.

I put my fingers in my mouth, still amazed at how good I taste.

CRYSTAL_TOY: Mmm. Your fingers taste so good, Mistress.

I suck and lick until my fingers are clean.

CRYSTAL_TOY: Thank You for allowing me the privilege.

MISTRESS_CIARA: Such a good pet. Understands her place. I sit you in my kitchen chair and walk behind you. I put a blindfold on you. How does it feel? Not too tight? Not too loose?

I don't own a blindfold, so I simply shut my eyes. I open one eye to type.

CRYSTAL_TOY: It's perfect. Thank You.

MISTRESS_CIARA: Good. I run My strong hands lightly down your face and your neck until I get to your chest. you feel Me standing behind you, pressing Myself against your back. My arms have your head secure between them as I reach down and grab your breasts, one in each hand. I knead your flesh like dough.

I close my eyes and can almost feel her pressing against me. I reach up and touch my breasts as if she were doing it. My breathing is becoming labored. This is so heady. This is not the same as passively watching Betlinde. This is active, and this woman, this Dominant named Mistress Ciara, is talking to me. *Me!*

CRYSTAL_TOY: Feels so good, Mistress. So good.

MISTRESS_CIARA: I stop kneading and pinch both nipples and hang on tight. I pinch tighter and then roll them around between My fingers.

I moan as I torture my nipples at her instruction.

CRYSTAL_TOY: Mmm…i'm moaning at Your touch, Mistress.

Typing is hard. I don't want to let my nipple go. My hand flies back to pinch myself more. There is a direct line from my nipples to my clit, and I am writhing in the chair.

MISTRESS_CIARA: I reach My hands down over your abdomen. I enjoy My superior dark skin against your pale. My fingers reach your shaved mons, and I run my hands back and forth over it. Yes, this is a truly smooth shave, pet. Good girl.

CRYSTAL_TOY: Thank you, Mistress.

I can't believe how hard I'm breathing as I rub my hands over myself.

MISTRESS_CIARA: I whisper in your ear - Spread your legs, pet.

I obey.

MISTRESS_CIARA: I reach down into your wetness.

I slide my fingers into my folds again.

MISTRESS_CIARA: My fingers are drenched from your excitement, pet. I insert them into your hole. I avoid your clit for now. I push in deep. I pull out. Push in, pull out. In, out. Increasing the pace.

CRYSTAL_TOY: MMM. So good.

I type this with one hand as I finger fuck myself with the other.

MISTRESS_CIARA: Yes, my pet likes to be fucked by her Mistress, doesn't she?

CRYSTAL_TOY: Yes. Yes. Yes, Mistress.

I type as fast as I can with my left hand. My right hand is buried deep inside me.

MISTRESS_CIARA: I plunge in hard and then stop all motion. My fingers are still buried in your cunt as I swivel your chair with you in it. I am now standing directly in front of you, between your wide-open legs.

My fingers point up inside you. I curl them and find your spongy tissue, your G-spot. I rub you slowly inside.

I follow her instructions and find the spongy soft tissue inside me. I rub slowly. Oh, God. This feels amazing. My apartment fades away. Mistress Ciara's fingers caressing my G-spot is the only thing I know. My ass lifts off the chair as I pull her fingers in deeper.

CRYSTAL_TOY: So goooood.

MISTRESS_CIARA: My pet likes My touch.

CRYSTAL_TOY: Yes.

MISTRESS_CIARA: Does My pet want to cum?

CRYSTAL_TOY: Yes, Mistress, yes. Please.

I am so ready to cum. It's building deep inside.

MISTRESS_CIARA: Not yet.

CRYSTAL_TOY: Ohhhhh.

I type this and say it at the same time.

MISTRESS_CIARA: With the fingers of My other hand, I circle your clit.

My body is shaking. Oh, God, I have never edged myself like this. It is bliss. It is torture.

CRYSTAL_TOY: Please.

Yes, I'm pleading.

MISTRESS_CIARA: Hold on, pet. Find a way. My fingers aren't done stroking My new pet's body. Exploring your silky wet cunt, your hard clit, your quaking white body.

I slow my fingers. It's the only way to stave off cumming. Somehow, she'll know if I blow too early.

MISTRESS_CIARA: My pet feels good? Doesn't she? she's riding high on My touch. Everything is centered in your cunt, isn't it, pet?

I yank my hand off my clit and smash the Y and enter keys. My hand flies back to my clit to continue the exquisite torture.

MISTRESS_CIARA: Such a good girl. Do it! Cum for Me, My pet. Do it for Me. Say My name when you cum. That's it. Feel it build, build.

My hips elevate on their own. My clit is swollen and stiff; it almost hurts. I arch my back and hold my breath as I slide into ecstasy. My inner walls crush my fingers. "Mistress Ciara," I say breathlessly and then moan as each wave hits. Holy fucking hell. The waves are still coming, coming, coming. After a few moments, I remember that I'm not the only one in on this. I look up at the screen and try to find Mistress Ciara's words.

I am still pulsing as I pull my fingers out and wipe them on a tissue. I wipe my other hand, too. I am a sticky mess. And the once-fresh towel underneath me is, once again, is a goner. I sit up. It takes all my strength, and I lay my head down on the desk and glance at the screen with one eye.

CRYSTAL_TOY: You've wrecked me.

MISTRESS_CIARA: Ahh, there's My pet. I thought I'd lost you.

CRYSTAL_TOY: Epic. Thank You, Mistress. Best! Orgasm! Ever!

MISTRESS_CIARA: Ever? Well, that's a nice compliment, My pet. This will take you far.

I want to close my eyes and float around the room, but I need water. I grab my glass and gulp down half of it.

CRYSTAL_TOY: Thank You.

MISTRESS_CIARA: Such a polite little pet. I'll need confirmation of this epic moment, though. This is a thing to be celebrated. Spread your legs, pet. Open your nether lips and take a pic of your weeping cunt. Send it to Me tonight. Keep one for yourself on your phone to commemorate this evening. The evening you officially became one of Mistress Ciara's pets.

CRYSTAL_TOY: i did?

It sounds like a fantastic thing, but I don't know what it means. I can't help the smile that is growing on my face. I wish she could see it.

CRYSTAL_TOY: Smiling big.

MISTRESS_CIARA: Good. I knew you were special. Send Me that pic, pet.

CRYSTAL_TOY: i will, Mistress. And thank You again. That was …

MISTRESS_CIARA: Mind-blowing. I know. I'm pretty damned wet over here Myself.

I want to ask her more. I want to ask her what she will do about her wet state, but I don't know how. I want to ask her who she is and how many human pets she has and where she works, and does she have children. But before I could even begin to put any words together, she sends me a message.

MISTRESS_CIARA: Does seven o'clock work for you on Wednesday evening, pet?

CRYSTAL_TOY: Yes, Mistress.

MISTRESS_CIARA: Good, and by the way, your orgasms are Mine now.

CRYSTAL_TOY: Meaning?

MISTRESS_CIARA: Meaning that you may play with yourself all you want, but you must not, under any circumstances, allow yourself to reach orgasm without My say so.

CRYSTAL_TOY: Oh.

MISTRESS_CIARA: Oh, what?

CRYSTAL_TOY: Oh, *Mistress*.

Jeez, I have to get with the program.

CRYSTAL_TOY: Wednesday is two days from now, Mistress. That's a long time to wait.

MISTRESS_CIARA: Lol. Good night, pet. I must get ready for My next appointment.

CRYSTAL_TOY: Good night, Mistress.

The high I was feeling is suddenly plummeting. Appointment? Was I her seven o'clock *appointment*? Does she have another for eight? An appointment with another woman going gaga over her? Just like me? I close my eyes; my head still lays on my desk. I am breathing heavily. Oh, God, what have I gotten myself into?

"Only the best friggin' orgasm of my entire life," I say out loud.

Chapter Five

Sweet Sweet Torture

When I wake up Tuesday morning, I am a little bit freaked out about what I did over the Internet with a stranger the night before, but a bigger part of me is oh so satisfied. It was the best sex I'd ever had. And even though I was alone, I wasn't. Mistress Ciara was there. Okay, she wasn't there physically, but she was definitely in my head.

And for some odd reason, I am super focused during my Calculus 1 lecture, and it goes uber smoothly. I even manage to work in a few algebra practice problems hoping to clear up my students' faulty skills, never belittling them in the process. I call it "Algebra Focus" and don't make a big deal of it. You can't reach students by making them feel stupid. That's counter-intuitive.

And I am just as focused as I bring my bag lunch into the break room to join the ladies who lunch.

"There she is," Miss Olga says. Everyone calls her Miss Olga. I'm not sure why. Maybe because she has the most prestigious position as the administrative assistant to Professor Wainwright, my department chair. "We missed you yesterday, Bernadette. Lucinda had pictures of her new grandbabies."

"Aww," I gush at Lucinda. "Let me see." I pull up a chair next to Lucinda. Her smile is so big, and her cheeks are rosy. She pulls her phone out of her pocket, pulls up the pictures, and hands it to me.

"Oh, no," I say, looking at two tiny new humans. "Twins?" I positively gush. "Your daughter had twins?"

She nods excitedly. Lucinda doesn't say much typically, but her excitement is real.

"Aww, have you seen them yet? No, they live in Texas or somewhere else, don't they?"

She frowns and says, "Thanksgiving."

"Oh, that's only a few weeks away. This will give your daughter and her husband time to get the hang of things before you get there, right?"

She nods once and grins. She must have had the same idea.

Miss Olga is positively beaming at me and my exchange with the ever-shy Lucinda. I always feel like a little girl under her gaze, and I feel warm all over, knowing that I have somehow pleased her.

The ladies who lunch pick up their conversation about the cute new photocopy repair guy, which gives me a moment to collect my thoughts. I have so far been successful keeping thoughts of Mistress Ciara at bay, but now that things are calm, I can't help but remember her standing behind me, touching me, telling me to open my legs wider. I feel my face getting red, and I stand up abruptly. Water. I find the mug Miss Olga gave me to use in the break room. It is a ceramic coffee mug with the red, blue, and white flag of Norway on it – the place where she was born. She hand wrote my name on a small piece of masking tape and slapped it on the bottom of the cup. This way everyone knows it belongs to me.

I fill up the mug at the water cooler and, still facing the wall, take a sip. I also take a deep breath and then let it out slowly. I force myself to think about a Fourier series computation using a simple piecewise function with infinite sums of sines and cosines. As I work out the mental calculations, it helps bring me back to earth. Feeling confident that my kinky life is no longer broadcasting, I turn around only to find five faces staring at me. Each one is sporting a knowing grin.

"What?" I say. My hand automatically goes up to my throat. It is a defensive gesture, and I know, absolutely know, that Miss Olga sees it for what it is.

"Spill," Miss Olga says simply. There is a twinkle in her eye as she says it.

I roll my eyes. Oh, my God. She knows. They all know. How can they know? *What* do they know? I meander back to the table and sit down.

"Who is she?" Miss Olga asks. The five sets of eyes are still riveted on me.

I feel my face turn oven-warm and know I am turning red. The smile creeping up my face also gives me away. I slowly move my sandwich out of the way and clunk my head on the table. It is my way of telling her that she is right but that I am embarrassed to talk about it.

"It's new?" Miss Olga asks.

"Yep," I say into the tabletop.

"So new that you don't want to talk about it yet?" Miss Olga suggests.

"Yep." I sit up but hide my smile behind a hand.

"Is she pretty?" Lucinda asks, causing everyone to look at her. Lucinda rarely joins in conversations. This is probably a first.

I think about Mistress Ciara's pictures and feel my face flush even more.

"Yep," I say to Lucinda and watch her smile widen. I move my hand to reveal my own smile.

"Does she make you happy?" Lucinda looks at me with her soft brown eyes.

I raise one eyebrow as I remember the cataclysmic orgasm Mistress Ciara had given me. "Yep," I say, not trusting myself to elaborate, mainly because I feel my face getting nuclear hot.

"Good. You deserve to be happy," Lucinda says and pats my forearm. She goes back to her lunch. It is the most I've ever heard her say in one sitting.

"What she said," Miss Olga says with a chuckle putting the final stamp on it. Which she always does. The other women voice their agreement with Lucinda's assessment, and then the subject turns back to the photocopy guy and his tight shirt and bulging biceps.

No more was said about my new love interest, but Miss Olga winks at me when I get up to head back to my office. I feel my nuclear blush return.

The Elementary Functions lecture goes well, as usual. Attendance is almost perfect, as it typically is for this class. I head straight home after the last student asks the last question. I make a quick stop to replenish my wine supply, and once home, I leave my clothes on and perv around *Kinks.com.* Instead of focusing on beautiful bodies, I read their writings. The home-grown erotica people post tempt me, but I get lost in the journal pieces. One of them is a user-created survey.

The title is *Are You Submissive?* Underneath that, there is a definition of submission as "humbly obedient and inclined to yield authority to others." Hmm, is that what being submissive is? Obedient? Yielding authority? I'm intrigued, so I read on and then decide to take the survey.

The survey asks you to evaluate yourself on twenty synonyms for the word submissive. Ahh, I see. They want you to rank yourself using a Likert scale. Five is *always,* four is *often,* three is *neutral,* two is *sometimes,* one is *rarely,* zero is *never.* It's not one of those online surveys that will total things up for you, so I get out a yellow legal pad and a mechanical pencil to do the arithmetic. Even though I am a mathematician, I don't trust my nerves to add the numbers in my head correctly.

I settle into my chair, the same chair in which the most epic orgasm of my life occurred, and I read the first word. *Meek,* four. I am often *Meek.* The next word is *Accommodating.* Five. I frown. Maybe I'm too accommodating. Jen is living in my three-bedroom, two-bath house that I own on five acres, and I am living here. How the fuck did she pull that one off? Why did I let her do that to me?

I take a deep breath and go through the rest of the words in turn. Deferential, Passive, Obedient, Dutiful, Abject, Amenable, Docile, Domesticated, Humble, Ingratiating, Lowly, Malleable, Menial, Obeisant, Obsequious, Patient, Pliable, Pliant.

The words *Abject* and *Lowly* make me mad, and I give them both resounding zeroes. I am neither of those things. *Patient, Dutiful, Amenable* – yes, perfect fives for these three.

I total up my score and see that I have a 74 out of a possible 100. According to the scoresheet, I am at the high end of the "Submissive" range, which covers 50-74. Apparently, I missed being a "Slave" by one point. The range 25-49 makes you a "Switch" – whatever that is, and 0-24 means you are a "Dominant."

"Hmm," I muse out loud. Seventy-four? Seriously? Am I that submissive? "No wonder a complete stranger could make me finger myself," I mumble. Mildly disturbed by the results, I wander into the kitchen for something to eat. I need to go shopping. I have plenty of wine, but I'm out of frozen pizzas. Microwave meal from a box it is.

I decide to ignore the survey results and go in search of some good erotica instead. There's a woman who writes hot stories on *Kinks*, so I search around until I find her again. Her ID is Rachels_toy. Let's see what Rachels_toy has to offer me tonight. Her profile has a cartoon of two girls kissing. It's cute. I click on her writings, and, holy moly, she has thirty-two pages filled with erotica and journal pieces. Some of them are over four years old. She's been around a while. I look at her profile. Oh, look, she has a series called "Begging for Discipline."

I click on "Begging for Discipline (Part 1)," and before I can even get past the title page, the microwave dings that my processed dinner is done being mutated by science. A glass of zinfandel accompanies my plastic food, and I settle into my chair to read.

> "Did you break that glass in the sink, slave?" The Domme who asked this question was wearing a black corset; her deep black hair piled high on her head. Her black-seamed stockings accentuated her shapely legs and drew your eye straight down to her five-inch red heels.

> The slave's nude body was draped face down over the end of her Domme's bed. She held her ass high to receive her lover's riding crop. The crop came down swiftly and without warning. It had obviously been unexpected, and the slave jumped with a whimper. "I'm sorry, Mistress. I didn't mean to break it."

> "Enough of your pitiful excuses, Muriel. You will now receive nineteen more strokes."

I read the story fast and furiously. The poor girl Muriel receives her strokes, and then her Domme orders her to roll over and spread her legs. The Domme runs the crop's handle through the folds of her slave's pussy, and it comes back wet. How can that be, I wonder? How can getting beaten like that make you wet and turned on? My father hit me with his belt one time for stealing candy from the Seven-Eleven when I was eight years old, and it hurt like hell. How could that be a turn-on?

I read more.

> "Thank You for disciplining me, Mistress," Muriel said breathlessly, her legs wide open, her wetness glistening. Her Domme's crop rhythmically stroked her nether regions. "I feel safe with You, Mistress." Muriel moaned and reached down to touch herself but quickly moved her hands to her thighs as if she knew her Domme would not allow it.

I laugh out loud. "At least I get to touch myself, Muriel," I tease the poor slave in the story, but then sober up immediately. "But you'll probably get to cum, won't you? Whereas I won't. Not until tomorrow night." I groan when I realize there is no guarantee that Mistress Ciara will even grant me an orgasm tomorrow night.

I squirm in my chair and feel a surge of wet heat down under. A lusty shudder runs through me. This is what a fetish is, isn't it? Something that makes your pussy surge at the mere thought of it? Mistress Ciara's Dominance. That's what's making me shudder. I unbutton my pants and pull the zipper down. Mistress Ciara said I was allowed to touch myself, so I reach in and slide my hand over my smooth stomach and mons.

I take a sharp breath when the tip of my middle finger discovers how exceptionally wet I am. I pull the wetness up to moisten my growing clit. Rachels_toy's erotica is turning me on but thinking about the hold Mistress Ciara has over me makes my nerves surge most delightfully.

I read the story on my screen and then close my eyes and imagine that I am the slave on the bed, legs opened wide. I stroke my clit and run my fingers through my wetness as I imagine the dildo that is presented to Muriel's waiting body is strapped on Mistress Ciara. She rubs it over my clit and asks if I can feel how hard she is. Mistress Ciara tells *me*, not Muriel, how I deserve to take the pounding she is about to give me because I broke the glass in the sink.

I leap up and shed my pants and boi shorts. I've been dressed for far too long. I search for my clear dildo stashed in the deep dark recesses of my desk and, after finding it, sit back in my chair, feet up on the desk, legs opened wide. I click the mouse to read more of the story.

The dildo is at the entrance of the slave's pussy. In one swift movement, the dildo is thrust inside and lays there "soaking." I feel the fullness of the silicone inside me. I have no idea what's happening with the slave in the story anymore because, in *my* story, Mistress Ciara pulls out slowly and then rams back into me, forcing my chair to rock. She does this again and again and again. My pussy clenches around the intrusion making it hard for her to pull the dildo out.

My hips arch. "Take me," I say to my imaginary Mistress. "Take me hard." And she does. I am moments away from the point of no return when I remember – I can't. Oh, God. This sucks. Mistress Ciara pulls out of me suddenly. I know she's laughing. All the way from Columbus, she's laughing at me. I groan. I feel empty. I am in agony. My sweet release has been denied. A surge of lust flashes through me, almost causing my body to orgasm on its own. I hold my breath and let the feeling pass. My eyes are closed. This is sweet, sweet torture. And she knew it would be.

Once I am no longer in danger of incinerating, I close the erotica story on my screen. I simply cannot take any more this evening. I will find out what happened to Muriel another day.

I bolt out of my command chair, not feeling in command of anything, and rinse off my dildo. I toss it in the top rack of the dishwasher. I fill the rest of the dishwasher with the dishes from the overflowing sink and then run it. I must remember to tuck the dildo away discretely before heading off to work in the morning. Not that anyone visits me in my apartment, but I need to stay ever-vigilant, especially now that my life seems to be taking this disturbing but deliciously kinky turn.

I laugh when I realize that I am not wearing a stitch of clothing down below. I need to shower and then just go to bed. That will make tomorrow and my date with Mistress Ciara come that much faster.

Lying in bed, I have a hard time falling asleep. I ask myself again what kind of game I've gotten myself into. And then I sit bolt upright when I wonder what kind of game Mistress Ciara is playing. She said she had an eight o'clock appointment. For money? Shit, is she going to want payment from me tomorrow evening? Is she going to ask for my credit card or a donation to her "charity" or something? Is she going to get me hooked on the power she has over me and then demand money? Is she a…? I can't for the life of me remember the word, but it is something like Money Dominant, a Dominant who requires cash and gifts in exchange for her services.

"Am I that desperate?" I say out loud to the darkness.

In my *Kinks.com* perusing this evening, I read about negotiations. I read that submissives and Dominants are supposed to discuss what each one expects of the relationship and their hard limits before anything happens between them. Mistress Ciara and I didn't have a conversation like that. Not yet, anyway. Maybe tomorrow night I'll ask her if she is a FinDomme. *FinDomme!* That's the word. But the thought of being so bold and demanding that we discuss limits makes me even more nervous than spreading my legs for her on command.

Am I willing to pay an anonymous woman to make love to me? *Make love?* I laugh at my choice of words. What happened last night was sex, pure and simple. So, am I? Am I willing to pay someone to have *sex* with me?

The question hangs heavy in my mind, mainly because it's not one that I can answer at the moment.

Chapter Six

"Y"

I am grateful I have no lectures today. It's Wednesday, and I've been hiding out in my office all morning planning lessons, answering emails, and grading problem sets. I'm hiding out mostly because of my foul mood. It's time for lunch, but I successfully avoid the ladies who lunch by claiming deadlines to Miss Olga when she stops by to walk with me to the break room. I prefer to brood alone, and I do so while eating my peanut butter and jelly sandwich on white bread at my desk. A nice side-effect of brooding, though, is that I have been productive. Part of me is beyond excited that I will be seeing Mistress Ciara later this evening, but another part of me is extremely disturbed by the question I still haven't been able to answer. Would I pay for online sex? If she asks me to pay tonight, will I? My rational brain says, "No fucking way," but that orgasm two nights ago? That can't be rationalized.

And not only am I disturbed by the fact that part of me might want to pay a stranger for sex, but I'm also equally disturbed by the fact that I sent that same stranger more pictures of my private parts. One of them was a wide-angle shot giving her my whole body – not my face, of course, but a nice torso shot from the neck down. It was kind of hot, if I do say so myself. It's even *Kinks* worthy, but I'm not brave enough to post that much of my body.

And this is another part of the reason I am in a foul mood. I don't know where those pictures will end up. I am not naïve enough to think the Internet is safe at all. But, apparently, I'm so desperate for attention that I'm willing to take the risk.

I look up at the analog clock on my office wall. My students always gasp when they see it. Instead of running the traditional clockwise, the numbers go the other way. The hands move from twelve to one by moving left instead of right. It helps remind me that some things can make perfect sense and function well but seem different and weird to those who've never experienced it. Most of my students shake their heads and reject it immediately without giving it a chance.

I stash the last of the Calculus 1 problem sets in my briefcase and lock up my office. I then head for the stairs for the department meeting. After the meeting, I plan on a quick stop at Kroger and then home. Being out of frozen pizzas has put me on edge. The word makes me pause, and my mind goes where it's been wanting to go all day. Edging. That's what Mistress Ciara did to me the other night. I was ready to cum, but she made me hold on until *she* was ready.

"Bernadette?" a voice startles me out of my thoughts. Dr. Wainwright is standing at the door to the conference room. "Are you coming?"

"Of course, of course," I stammer. My head was so far in the clouds that I had walked right past the meeting. "Just getting a quick sip of water." I gesture toward a water fountain down the hallway.

"We're starting in five," he says curtly and goes in the room.

I start to turn around to follow him, the water was a lie anyway, but then I get mad. To simply turn around at his implied command would be like giving in, and with the anti-social mood I'm in, I don't feel like giving in. I do, however, quicken my pace to the water fountain. I take a quick sip and then head back to the conference room. I smile at Miss Olga, who has her laptop open and is ready to take the meeting minutes. I take my usual seat in the far corner in the back of the room and settle in.

I barely register the usual nuts and bolts crap, preferring to doodle fractals on the agenda sheet. Dr. Wainwright announces the dates that final grades are due, the last official date for course evaluations, and more crap like that. Who cares? Send me an email. Miss Olga will get all that down in her notes anyway, and we'll all have a copy tomorrow morning first thing.

My ears perk up when he mentions courses for the spring and summer terms. I am listening now. Priority will be given to full and associate professors. I frown. I'm still an assistant professor. Tenured, yes, but on the lowest end of the totem pole. I have to make more of a name for myself in my field before they even consider me for an associate professorship. And just because the university focuses on teaching doesn't mean I don't want to do research. I do. I want to contribute to refereed journals. I just need a chance. I feel like my career is passing me by because asshole Wainwright won't give me a break. I will be sure to get my requests to him early, tomorrow probably. I need him to understand that I seriously want to be considered for the graduate-level courses. I'd like to move out of the freshman business and into some serious mathematics. And even though I may not get what I want for the spring term, I hope to get some higher-level courses next year. I have to or else. I laugh because I have no earthly idea what the "or else" would entail.

I look back down at my doodling. One of these days, I will muster up the courage to demand recognition for taking on the courses that no one else wants. And I'm going to demand that I get rewarded.

The meeting adjourns, and I grab my briefcase without looking back. I don't even say goodbye to Miss Olga. That will get me in trouble with her tomorrow, but I just can't face her right now. She reads me like a book, and with my new internet "hobby," I'm not ready to be read like a book. I head directly home and don't bother going to Kroger. I can't. I can't see people, not while I'm in this mood. I have an overwhelming need to throw things. I don't want to risk being rude to a cashier or one of those moms with screaming kids or some old geezer blocking the aisle with his cart. I can't be with people right now because I'm sliding down some kind of rabbit hole of my own making.

Once inside my apartment, I take the hottest shower I can stand. Afterward, I dry off and can't look myself in the mirror. I don't particularly understand who I am at the moment or who I am becoming. I don't bother getting dressed and simply throw myself into bed nude. I set my alarm for six pm and lay down for a nap. One hour should give me time to snarf my last frozen microwave meal before meeting Mistress Ciara at seven. Sleep comes blessedly quickly.

~~~

I wake up refreshed. Good. I wasn't sure if my funk was going to stay with me. How could it? I have a date with my Mistress in an hour. "My Mistress," I say out loud, trying it on to see how it feels. Chills run through me. The words feel right. Even though I know Mistress Ciara won't see my face or hair, I still brush it to get the bedhead out of it. My stupid cowlick is giving me trouble, so I take an extra minute to attempt to get it to obey.

Obey. That's a funny word. I *obeyed* Mistress Ciara's command *not* to reach orgasm yesterday after reading Rachels_toy's erotica. I obeyed her by using that wacky capitalization scheme to show her respect. And I will obey her this evening by announcing myself five minutes before our scheduled time as she requested.

Finally satisfied with my hair, I pad through the living room and then into the kitchen in my birthday suit. I stop as my feet hit the cold kitchen tile. All this nudist colony stuff is fine, but what if I get a package delivered or the property manager or a neighbor knocks on the door? I should have a robe handy. I rush back into my bedroom and grab it. I purchased it when I was living with Jen. I'd put it on after a shower, so she wouldn't have to see my naked body. It was like we had become roommates or something and not life companions, which is what I thought we were. Apparently not. And why is everything reminding me of her now? I turn the Jen switch off in my head.

I toss the robe on the couch near the front door and, before turning back to the kitchen, wonder how soundproof my front door is. I can't take any more chances, so I stuff some blankets along the bottom. I sneak a peek out the eyehole and see nothing but my dark corner of the dimly lit hallway. I heard once about people spying on you through those peepholes, so I grab my trusty post-it-notes and cover it thoroughly.

I head back into the kitchen, and once my microwave meal is finished nuking, I take it and a large glass of ice water to my desk. I don't trust myself with wine tonight. I need to be clear-headed. I power up my computer and tool around *Kinks.com* for a while, waiting for 6:55 pm. I click open Rachels_toy's story about the poor submissive named Muriel, who broke the glass and is now getting punished. I should have known better than to feel sorry for her. Muriel is having the time of her life. Not only does her Mistress fill her pussy with the dildo and bring her to a screaming orgasm, but then the Mistress turns her over. The dildo is lubed up and pressed against Muriel's backdoor. I close my eyes for a moment and cringe. I know and understand that people have anal sex. But, c'mon, seriously? Do they seriously like being penetrated that way? Or are they merely trying to please their partners by allowing them to do that?

"Don't judge," I say out loud. There are a lot of fetishes I know nothing about. Anal sex is one of them.

I open my eyes feeling brave enough to read on.

> The Mistress smiled as she pressed the sheening dildo to her submissive's other hole. She will never let Muriel see her satisfied smile because it is one of pride. She is proud that her submissive can take whatever is dished out, proud that her submissive obeys and complies with her every command. She is proud of the work they've done together to hone their D/s relationship.
>
> The Mistress leaned forward, applying a bit more pressure as she grabbed her sub's hips firmly. Muriel moaned in anticipation. The Mistress pressed harder

and all at once gained an inch of access. Muriel's head lowered toward the bed and stifled a groan.

"Take it, slave," the Mistress commanded. "Take your punishment as I enjoy your body."

"Yes, Mistress," Muriel said breathlessly. The accompanying moan betrayed the fact that she did not find this to be a punishment at all. "Take me, Mistress. Use me. Fuck me."

The Mistress pushed in slowly but unrelentingly. She continued her assault until the entire dildo disappeared into Muriel's body.

I slide my hand down my torso and am just about to touch myself when I notice the time on the lower right-hand side of my computer screen. "Shit, shit, shit," I say in a panic. It's one minute before seven. I quickly switch over to the mail system and click on our chat link.

CRYSTAL_TOY: I am here, Mistress Ciara.

My heart is pounding. I almost blew it. I take a few deep breaths, willing my heart to slow down. I stare at the screen like a lovesick puppy. Oh, shit, I didn't use a lowercase i. Dammit.

There is no immediate response, and at 7:05, I wonder if I should send another message alerting her to the fact that I am there and that I'm waiting for her. I put my fingers to the keyboard but then wonder what I would say. My first message says it all. I am here.

I stand up. I pace. Every time I pass the computer screen, I look to see if she has responded. She hasn't. All this nervous energy has me feeling like I have to pee. With a glance at the screen, I see there is no message and decide to chance it. I run to the bathroom, pee, and hurry back to my desk. And there it is, her reply.

MISTRESS_CIARA: Are you wet, pet?

CRYSTAL_TOY: Yes, Ma'am.

MISTRESS_CIARA: Did you get yourself off?

CRYSTAL_TOY: No.

I decide to keep it simple.

MISTRESS_CIARA: Do you *want* to get off?

Her reply came swiftly.

CRYSTAL_TOY: Yes, Mistress.

My reply also comes swiftly.

MISTRESS_CIARA: Good answer, pet. Got your dildo handy?

CRYSTAL_TOY: Yes, Mistress.

I type that and then dive into my desk drawer. I reach for the dildo in the back, where it is usually stashed. Panic rises in my core when I can't find it. It's not in or *on* my desk. I gasp when I realize that it is still in the dishwasher. I leap up and scurry to the kitchen. I yank open the dishwasher and pull out the top rack. I groan in relief as I grab the now-clean two-headed dildo and race back to my chair.

On the screen is her reply.

> MISTRESS_CIARA: Good. Strip and get on your knees
> before Me, slave.

Slave? I am not a slave, but now is not the time for arguing. I move off my chair and get on my knees. I struggle to find a comfortable position. Kneeling is not a natural position for me. Next time I will have a pillow handy. I pull the laptop to the edge of the desk so that I can respond.

> CRYSTAL_TOY: Done, Mistress. i kneel before You.

> MISTRESS_CIARA: Good girl, so obedient.

My cheeks grow warm, but I don't know what to type, so I don't type anything.

> MISTRESS_CIARA: I reach down and fasten a collar
> around your neck. I attach a black leather leash to the
> collar.

I don't have a collar, but I reach up and press my thumb and index finger of my left hand around my neck to feel something.

> MISTRESS_CIARA: I take the loose end of the leash
> and run it gently across your eager face. you feel the
> leather touch your cheek, your chin, your lips.

I don't know why, but a wave of lust runs through me at her words.

> MISTRESS_CIARA: Open your mouth, pet.

CRYSTAL_TOY: i open it.

MISTRESS_CIARA: I lay the strap long ways across your bottom teeth. Bite down and feel the leather.

I have no leash, but I pull out a leather bookmark from my top desk drawer and put that in my mouth. I bite down as asked.

MISTRESS_CIARA: And now you tangibly feel My control over you. you feel My power. you feel My Dominance.

CRYSTAL_TOY: Yes, Mistress, i do.

MISTRESS_CIARA: I pull the leash from your mouth abruptly and, without warning, yank you to your feet.

Oh, thank God. I grab onto the desk and pull myself up. My legs were starting to get pins-and-needles in that kneeling position.

MISTRESS_CIARA: I reach down and slide my fingers through your folds. you're wet, pet.

CRYSTAL_TOY: Yes, Ma'am.

MISTRESS_CIARA: What made you wet?

I can't tell her that reading erotica made me wet, even though it did, so I tell her a partial truth.

CRYSTAL_TOY: You made me wet. Thinking of You and Your Dominance, Mistress. i am wet for You.

MISTRESS_CIARA: Good, pet. So compliant. So eager. I pull you by the leash and lead you to one of My favorite places here in My living room.

I gasp. She's picturing me there with her.

MISTRESS_CIARA: See that couch?
I look over at mine.

CRYSTAL_TOY: Yes, Mistress. It's lovely.

I shrug. I don't know why I added that last part.

MISTRESS_CIARA: LOL. Yes, it is lovely. And it will look even more lovely with you bent over the back of it.

CRYSTAL_TOY: What will You do with me once i'm bent over it, Mistress?

MISTRESS_CIARA: So eager. you are a lovely pet. Let's find out, shall W/we?

CRYSTAL_TOY: Yes, please.

MISTRESS_CIARA: I lead you to the back of the couch and slam your thighs and hips against it. Bend forward, pet. Bend over the top and present your sex to your Mistress.

CRYSTAL_TOY: Yes, Ma'am.

I look over at my thrift store couch and realize it's too far away from the computer. I drape myself over my desk instead. It is a little low but will suffice for now.

MISTRESS_CIARA: I jam two fingers into your cunt. you are saturated with slickness.

CRYSTAL_TOY: For You, Mistress.

I groan with pleasure as I pump two fingers in and out of my wetness.

MISTRESS_CIARA: I wipe My wet fingers on your naked ass cheeks. You are My plaything, My toy, and I can do with you whatever I want. And what I want is to fuck you from behind while you're draped over My couch. I want to hear you moan, crystal_toy. I want to hear you groan. I want to hear you scream My name when you cum and beg for mercy when I don't stop fucking you with My big black cock even after you've cum.

Her words hit me viscerally. My body tremors with pure lust. My pussy aches to be filled. I tell her so.

CRYSTAL_TOY: Fuck me, Mistress. i am Yours. Do what You want with me.

MISTRESS_CIARA: I nudge your legs wider apart. Using both hands, I pull your thighs apart even further to see My treasure. Your cunt belongs to Me, slave. Open it for Me. Open your white-girl cunt. Reach down and part those lips so I can see your slick cavern.

Even though I am alone, I am utterly self-conscious as I reach through my legs with one hand and spread my inner lips for her.

CRYSTAL_TOY: So wet for You.

I say this and type it at the same time.

MISTRESS_CIARA: Feel my BBC poking at the entrance.

I reach for my dildo and place it there.

CRYSTAL_TOY: You're so big, Mistress.

MISTRESS_CIARA: I push in slowly, about an inch, and pull back out.

I mimic her commands.

MISTRESS_CIARA: I push back in even further, a full three inches this time.

It is heavenly.

MISTRESS_CIARA: I pull back and then slam fully into you. your hips grind against My couch.

I plunge my dildo in as far as it will go. I feel my upper thighs smash against my wooden desk. I am glad the edges are rounded. My pussy clenches the dildo tight.

MISTRESS_CIARA: I pump out and in. In and out. Slow. A nice steady pace.

CRYSTAL_TOY: Feels so good, Mistress.

I can barely type at this point. Her dildo inside me feels so good.

MISTRESS_CIARA: I pick up the pace. A nice medium pace, but steady and smooth. you are entertaining My BBC in your body for the first time, slave. you must revere this moment.

CRYSTAL_TOY: Smooth. Big. Full.

That's all I have to offer. My breathing is getting heavy as she pounds me.

MISTRESS_CIARA: Faster now, pet. Faster. I am slamming into your body. Fucking you because I want to because I can, because you are My toy. Does crystal_toy belong to Me?

CRYSTAL_TOY: Yes. Yes. Yes, i belong to You.

I barely get the words typed because she's slamming into me from behind. My orgasm is building from somewhere deep inside. A secret nerve is getting hit over and over and over. I feel it rising.

CRYSTAL_TOY: Can't hold on, M.

I accidentally hit the enter key before finishing her title.

MISTRESS_CIARA: Oh, but you will. Another little while. BBC is just getting Her groove on fucking a little white toy bent over the couch. Fucking you hard, hard, hard.

My dildo thrusts in and out so hard that I almost can't take it.

CRYSTAL_TOY: Have to cum, Mistress. Pleez.

I barely notice my misspelling.

MISTRESS_CIARA: One more minute. BBC hasn't had a good workout with a fine female toy in ages. She loves a good cunt to play in.

I groan and relax into the pounding I am getting. My eyes are closed as I ride the wave of ecstasy that is building to higher heights than I've ever known.

MISTRESS_CIARA: BBC's ready to cum inside you, pet. Cum with Her. Cum with My BBC. Cum, pet. Cum for your Mistress. Cum for Me.

I let the tension go, and my orgasm builds. All at once, there is nothingness as if I've been thrown into outer space. I bask in the stillness until a mad rushing hurtles me back into reality. "Mistress! Mistress Ciara! Ciara," I cry out as I cum. I slow my dildo's speed. My body spasms around the silicone cylinder over and over and over.

CRYSTAL_TOY: Cummmmmm.

I have been silent on my end for a while.

CRYSTAL_TOY: Sp gppd.

Spelling is out the window. Who cares?

MISTRESS_CIARA: BBC is pleased. And when She's pleased, She pumps. Keep pumping Her, pet. Keep pumping.

I groan. My inner walls are contracting so deliciously that I just want to bask in the feeling. I do as I'm told, though, and slide my dildo in and out. Unbelievably, I feel myself peaking again.

CRYSTAL_TOY: Mmmmm.

It's as coherent as I can be at the moment.

MISTRESS_CIARA: Keep pumping. BBC wants another one from you. When you cum, say My name, pet. Say My name.

My breathing is ragged. My arm pumps the dildo without my conscious knowledge. I am hauled up the mountain, and without warning, I am thrown off. I freefall and call her name as I cum,

"Mistresssssssssssss. Oh, fuck, fuck, fuck, fuck, fuck, fuck." I collapse on the desk. The dildo slides out of me and lands somewhere on the carpeted floor. I don't care. I am flying. My eyes are closed as I ride the heavens. I am nowhere and everywhere at once.

My eyes shoot wide open when I hear a noise outside in the hallway. My heart pounds from adrenaline. Is someone here? I hear voices. Oh, my God, It's just my neighbors. Their door slams like it always does when they come home. I put a hand to my chest and sit down in my chair. I laugh when I see the message on my screen.

MISTRESS_CIARA: Is My pet all right?

CRYSTAL_TOY: More than all right, Mistress. That was amazing.

MISTRESS_CIARA: My BBC loves fresh cunt, pet. Did you say My name?

CRYSTAL_TOY: Yes, Mistress. Each time. The universe heard me, i think.

MISTRESS_CIARA: That's My good girl.

I beam.

CRYSTAL_TOY: Thank You. i try.

MISTRESS_CIARA: W/we need to talk business.

My eyes shoot open wide. Oh, God. Here it is. The FinDomme emerges.

CRYSTAL_TOY: Okay.

MISTRESS_CIARA: I want to meet you.

Mistress Ciara's message sits there on the screen like a thing unknown.

I can't think of a thing to say in response. No one can know who I am. She knows I don't live in Antarctica, but she has no idea where I live unless she has computer spy skills or something.

> MISTRESS_CIARA: I saw the Cincinnati Bengals hat, pet. In one of the lovely pictures you sent Me. you're a Cin-City girl, aren't you?

I am floored. I fucked up. I wasn't thinking clearly when I took those pictures. Shit, shit, shit. My cover is blown. I focus on breathing. And then an idea comes to me. I won't answer her.

> MISTRESS_CIARA: your silence is answer enough, pet. Come to Columbus. I want to buy you dinner. Just dinner and conversation. That's all. you'll tell friends where you're going. you can check in with them every hour. I will insist on that for your safety. your Mistress would like to see where O/our meeting might take U/us.

I can't respond. I am frozen stiff.

> MISTRESS_CIARA: your secret will be safe, pet. I take care of all My slaves. you don't even have to tell Me your real name. Ever.

My eyes are riveted on the cursor blinking in the space where I am supposed to type my reply. I can't move.

> MISTRESS_CIARA: How about next Wednesday. The day before Thanksgiving?

I am aghast as I watch myself reach for the keyboard and type the capital letter "Y." As if mind controlled, I reach over and press the enter button. I am stunned. Oh, God, what have I done?

Chapter Seven

As Confused as Ever

Thursday comes, and I fly through my classes with blinders on. I am laser-beam focused on each task at hand. This way, my mind won't wander into parts of my life that I can't deal with at the moment. One student drops by during my office hours, and I help her understand the complexities of optimization using differential calculus. She seems to get it, and I am grateful for the distraction. I do, however, wonder what she would think if she knew I was a sexual deviant. I close my eyes and take a deep breath. I let it out slowly. I cannot go down that road. I must keep Mistress Ciara and her request at bay. Not losing my shit is the paramount goal today.

I stand up abruptly, pack my briefcase, and scoot out of the Mathematics building. The thought of Miss Olga stopping by jangles my nerves too much. She'd know something was wrong and might get it out of me. She's that good, and I'm that weak.

I put the heater on in the car. November has decided to become winter all of a sudden. I stop at the Kroger near the apartment and stock up on frozen pizzas, wine, microwave meals, and bottled waters. I know I should get fruits and vegetables, but I just don't.

Once I am home and the groceries are put away, I shower to clear my head. As I stand under the streaming water, all the thoughts I'd been holding back all day come flooding out. My heart clenches.

"Oh, my God," I say out loud and smack the tile with the side of my fist. "What did I fucking do? She knows where I live. My life is over." The tears that I'd held back all day bubble up and spill over. The shower water washes away my tears as soon as they appear, but I cannot stop the emotional outpouring for the life of me.

Once I can finally take a deep breath, I stand up tall, determined not to wither away into nothingness, and then calmly finish my shower. The water has run cold. Yeah, that's fitting. A cold shower is what I should have done before setting foot in that kinky website.

I step out of the shower, shivering. I grab my sheet towel and wrap up in it. As fast as I can, I pull on sweats and a sweatshirt and wooly socks. I shiver because I'm cold, but there is an underlying cause for my shivers – I'm scared. And angry. I'm angry at myself for not having the guts to tell Mistress Ciara that no, I will not drive to Columbus to meet her. And I'm angry that I didn't come up with a lie to explain the Bengals hat. As I sit on the edge of my bed, rubbing the worry lines off my forehead, I realize that I'm also angry at myself for not having the guts to relax and enjoy being wanted. To enjoy being a sexual creature and enjoy being excited about maybe having sex with a real live woman.

"When did I become a fucking Puritan, anyway?" I ask the empty room. This is what I had always accused Jen of being. Not to her face, of course. Just quietly in my mind. "It's a date. That's all." My empty room is not convinced. I am not swayed, either, because I realize that sex might not even be on the table if I were to drive up there.

Sex on the table? I grin as I picture Mistress Ciara sweeping the plates off the restaurant table and taking me with her BBC as I lay draped face down over the edge. A surge of lust shoots through me, and I close my eyes at the vision. I groan. What am I? A teenage boy? What is up with these overactive hormones? Jeez.

With a start, I realize that all is not lost. I don't have to meet Mistress Ciara. I don't have to show my face to her. Ever. In fact, I never have to talk to her again. Ahh, but who am I kidding? I have an online date with her tonight. Laughing, I stand up and head for my computer in the living room. Even though she kind of knows I live in Cincinnati, she doesn't know exactly where. She doesn't know what I do for a living. In short, she doesn't know who I am at all.

And I kind of want to continue this life-altering online thing we have. I can't call it a relationship, can I? I have no idea. But I have to figure something out about her request to meet me in person. Will I, or won't I? That is the question. I'm leaning toward won't.

One frozen pizza and a half bottle of wine later, it is almost 5:00. I have two whole hours to kill before meeting my Mistress. I finish grading the Calculus problem sets and get a good start on the Elementary Functions sets. Some professors rely solely on online homework platforms, and I use those in a limited fashion, but students need personalized one-on-one feedback. And this, in my humble opinion, can only be done effectively with handwritten assignments.

Feeling good about one part of my life at least, I decide to spend time reading more of Rachels_toy's series about Muriel and her Domme. I was almost finished with Part One of her *Begging for Discipline* series, so I click that open. After reading for a titillating fifteen minutes, I am nicely turned on and ready for Part Two. I don't hesitate and click open the next story. I laugh because poor Muriel is in a bind again, but this time literally.

Muriel wore wrist and ankle cuffs. Her arms were spread overhead, and her legs spread below as her Domme bound her to the St. Andrew's cross. The blindfold over her eyes deprived her of sight. She heard her Domme moving nearby but did not know what her punishment would be this time.

"So many things left undone, Muriel," the Domme singsonged gently. "You must learn to take care of details. How hard is it to use a feather duster?"

Muriel's sharp intake of breath had the desired effect when a feather lightly caressed her face. The soft feather moved lower to her breasts and lingered there, teasing her nipples hard. She squirmed when the super-soft object teased an inner elbow and then moved to the pit under her arm. If there had been no blindfold, her Domme would have seen Muriel's eyes rolling up into her head as she was slowly and sensuously tortured.

All at once, the feather disappeared. Muriel strained to hear where her Domme was. A single finger was thrust into her dripping pussy, making her gasp. The finger spread her wetness to cover her enlarged clit.

"So erect, Muriel. This clit is out of control. Let's give her something to think about." Her Domme's finger circled and circled the growing member. Abruptly, the finger was taken away. Muriel cried out at the loss.

Within seconds, the Domme's finger was back. But the finger was cold this time. A blast of sensation quickly spread over Muriel's clit.

"A little peppermint oil for her," Muriel's Domme said. "This will teach her to behave."

Muriel squirmed in her restraints. Her breathing quickened as the hot yet cold sensation deepened and spread.

I don't know what it is about this story or how it's written, but it sure gets me hot and stimulated. I am bundled up in my cold apartment, but I slide my hand down below and find wet and swollen pussy lips. I rub my clit slowly as I read, letting my excitement build. And just as my orgasm is heading to the point of no return, I stop. I close my eyes and ride the heady wave of firing nerve endings. Will my Mistress tip me over tonight? Will her words dance in my brain and travel south to stimulate me there? I grip the arms of my chair as a wave of hot lust rushes through me at the thought of her.

I have to stop thinking about her. I have to stop thinking about Muriel and her Domme. I need a distraction. You know what? I should send the writer a message. I should tell Rachels_toy how hot her stories are and how well-written. I will share the love.

I find Rachels_toy's *Kinks.com* page again and click on the message icon. It takes me several minutes to find the right words to compliment her without sounding like a lecherous creep. I tell her how I accidentally stumbled on her story, but now I am hooked on Muriel always getting in trouble with her Domme. And how delectably - yes, I use the word delectably – her Domme deals with the transgressions. Satisfied with my message, I hit the send icon. I check the time and see that I have an hour and a little to go before date time.

I click back onto Muriel's story, but before I even read two sentences, I see the mail icon light up. Momentary panic squeezes my stomach. Am I late for Mistress Ciara? Is she canceling? I zip my mouse up to the icon and click. Relief floods through me. Rachels_toy responded to me. Maybe it's one of those automatic replies. The kind that says, "Thank you for your message. I will get back to you when I can."

I click it open. And I am shocked to see it is *not* an automatic reply.

RACHELS_TOY: Thank you so much for the high praise of my writing. It is always fun connecting with people who read my stuff. I'm glad you're enjoying the series. How far have you read?

Really? Does she want to chat with me? Wait. Is she a Dominant? I quickly hit the link for her profile page and scan it. Ahh, no. She is a submissive. Oh, duh. Her *Kinks* name is Rachels_toy. That probably means someone named Rachel is her Dominant.

I head back to the mail icon and hit reply.

> CRYSTAL_TOY: I am halfway through Part 2 of *Begging for Discipline.* Do you think that Muriel messes up on purpose? You know – to get her Mistress to discipline her?

> RACHELS_TOY: Oh, definitely. Most of the time, anyway. Like me, sometimes Muriel's a klutz, and it's accidental.

I read her message and smile. It's so cool to have immediate access to a writer like this. Before I can craft a reply, she sends me another message.

> RACHELS_TOY: You're pretty new around here, aren't you?

> CYRSTAL_TOY: Yes…I've already been scooped up by a Mistress.

> RACHELS_TOY: Fresh meat! LOL! I'm just kidding, but kind of not. Just be careful. There are wolves in here, and they are sometimes very crafty about hiding who they really are.

Her statement gives me pause, and, in a flood, I find myself confiding in her. I tell her that my Mistress wants to meet me and that she somehow found out that I lived sort of close to her and that I can't reveal my identity for fear of repercussions jobwise. I don't know why I trusted Rachels_toy so quickly, because who knows, maybe *she* is one of those wolves.

> RACHELS_TOY: Okay. Answer this. *Do* you want to meet her?

I take a deep breath and look up at nothing.

> CRYSTAL_TOY: I don't know. Actually, I think I *do* want to meet her.

I cringe at my boldness. Is this true? Do I really want to meet her? Yes. Yes, I think I do.

> RACHELS_TOY: Well, then. Here's what we need to do.

I like that she takes me under her wing. We talk about the logistics of going up there. She says that I absolutely have to tell someone where I am going and when. She volunteers to be one of those people but says that I need someone here at home to be a point of contact. I know who I am going to tell, with limited details, of course – Miss Olga. Rachels_toy suggests that I tell my local contact that I am going on a date. That's all they need to know. There is no need to reveal where I'd met her initially.

> RACHELS_TOY: But I want you to update me as well. Just shoot me a message here on *Kinks*. Do you have the *Kinks* app for your phone?

When I tell her that I don't, she walks me through downloading it, and then I practice using it by messaging her on my phone. It is awesome, and I feel very connected with her. I tell her so.

> RACHELS_TOY: I'm glad you found me, Crystal. Hey, can we at least exchange first names? I don't need your last name, but if something goes sideways, I at least want to be able to tell the police your first name.
>
> CRYSTAL_TOY: Police?

Now she has me really worried.

> RACHELS_TOY: It won't come to that. I checked out your Mistress's page, and she seems pretty legit. But you never know, right? It's better to be prepared.

I cringe at her words.

> CRYSTAL_TOY: This whole thing sounds so daunting. I like your suggestion about thinking of it as a date.
>
> RACHELS_TOY: Good. My name's Lisa, btw.

I hesitate, but just for a moment, and then type my real name.

> CRYSTAL_TOY: Bernadette.
>
> RACHELS_TOY: It's nice to meet you, Bernadette. Okay, here's what you'll need to do on the day of your date.

And from there, Lisa gives me all kinds of good advice like bringing enough cash to pay for dinner if Mistress Ciara reneges on her offer to pay. Don't use a credit card because I won't know who will see it and abuse it. Call Miss Olga as soon as I get to the restaurant to let her know that I made it there. Contact Lisa every hour after that and then contact Miss Olga when I get ready to go home or stay over. I balk a little, no a lot, at the stay over part, but put on my big girl pants and allow the possibility to enter my mind.

The alarm on my phone makes me jump, and through the pounding of my heart, I let Lisa know that I have to get ready for my online date with my Mistress.

> RACHELS_TOY: Have fun! I, myself, am going to see what other types of mischief our little Muriel can get herself into.
>
> CRYSTAL_TOY: I can't wait! Thanks for your help. I'm glad I contacted you.
>
> RACHELS_TOY: Me, too. I like helping newbies. One day I'll tell you the story about how I was led down the aisle on a leash the day I married Rachel.
>
> CRYSTAL_TOY: No way!
>
> RACHELS_TOY: Yes, way. Now, go! Go get ready.
>
> CRYSTAL_TOY: Thanks again.

She doesn't respond, so I jump up out of my chair to hit the bathroom and put my dinner trash away. I pour myself another glass of wine and then grab a pillow off the couch just in case I will be kneeling later. I secure my windows, soundproof my door, and toss my robe on the couch. I open up the mail chat I have going with my Mistress.

CRYSTAL_TOY: i'm here, Mistress.

MISTRESS_CIARA: I'm glad, My pet. How are you feeling?

CRYSTAL_TOY: Happy now that You're here.

Oh, God, I'm pathetic.

MISTRESS_CIARA: What are you wearing?

Nothing like getting right down to business.

CRYSTAL_TOY: Sweats and a sweatshirt.

MISTRESS_CIARA: Panties?

CRYSTAL_TOY: Yes.

MISTRESS_CIARA: Yes, *what*?

I can believe I forgot her title.

CRYSTAL_TOY: Yes, Mistress. I'm sorry for the mistake.

MISTRESS_CIARA: And you just made your second.

CRYSTAL_TOY: I did?

MISTRESS_CIARA: And your third. you must be punished, pet.

Oh, my God. Autocorrect keeps changing my lowercase i to a capital I. What the hell?

CRYSTAL_TOY: i'm sorry, Mistress. i was inattentive to my capitalization. i deserve whatever punishment You deem appropriate for me.

I hit send on my message, wondering what the hell is about to happen to me.

MISTRESS_CIARA: Do you have nipple clips, pet?

CRYSTAL_TOY: No, Mistress.

MISTRESS_CIARA: Clothespins or bobby pins?

CRYSTAL_TOY: No, Mistress. Neither of those.

MISTRESS_CIARA: That's okay. W/we can improvise. I'm fairly certain you have chip clips for snack foods. you'll need all that you can find. And do you have wooden spoons?

CRYSTAL_TOY: Yes, i have several different wooden spoons and a dozen or more clips.

MISTRESS_CIARA: Excellent. Go on. Go fetch.

She says this as if I'm a dog, but apparently, I'm not insulted by it and do as I'm told and hurry to the kitchen junk drawer.

CRYSTAL_TOY: Fifteen bag clips, Mistress

MISTRESS_CIARA: Lovely. Eliminate the ones with jagged teeth. I want to punish you, not hurt you.

"Oh," I say out loud, and it is only at this moment in time that I realize what she intends to do with these clips. My breathing gets shallow. I'm not sure I am like Muriel. I'm not sure that I'm into pain. I guess I'm about to find out.

CRYSTAL_TOY: i have six clips without teeth.

MISTRESS_CIARA: And the spoons?

CRYSTAL_TOY: i have three. All different sizes.

CRYSTAL_TOY: Mistress.

I can't believe I forget her title. I might be in bigger trouble now.

MISTRESS_CIARA: Good save, pet. This is excellent. Now tell Me your transgressions.

CRYSTAL_TOY: i didn't use Your honorific when i addressed You, Mistress.

MISTRESS_CIARA: And that is a sign of disrespect. I can't have My pets running around disrespecting Me, now can I?

CRYSTAL_TOY: No, Mistress.

MISTRESS_CIARA: They don't last long as My pets if they do. Is that understood?

CRYSTAL_TOY: Yes, Ma'am.

I have no idea why, but her words send shots of excitement through me. I squirm in my chair and feel how wet I am becoming.

MISTRESS_CIARA: What else did you do incorrectly, crystal_toy?

CRYSTAL_TOY: i disrespected Your superiority my not checking my capitalization. i should be lower than You at all times. This way, i show You that i know my place.

There, I think smugly. I let *her* know that *I* know who's in charge. She is.

MISTRESS_CIARA: Excellent answer. Now, first of all, shed those clothes. Let Me know when this is done.

I leap up and pull off my sweatshirt and t-shirt. I shiver as the cool apartment air hits my naked torso. As I'm wrestling off my sweatpants, I shimmy over to the thermostat and raise the heat. Once relieved of my pants, I stretch and then sprint back to my waiting Mistress.

CRYSTAL_TOY: my task is complete, Mistress.

MISTRESS_CIARA: That was quick. Good girl. Get one of those chip clips ready. First, put your index finger and thumb of your right hand into your mouth and get them nice and wet. Run them over your right nipple, making her nice and firm. Take a clip and gently attach it to your erect nipple. Ahh, that's it, pet. Bask in the pain that gives so much sweet, sweet pleasure.

As soon as the clip closes on my nipple, I gasp at the pain. My eyes slam shut as the pain waves ripple through me and head straight to my clit. My breathing quickens, and I hear myself moan. *This is exquisite*, I think and then type those exact words to my Mistress.

MISTRESS_CIARA: Good. My pet understands pain. But W/we're not done. Harden the other nipple with wet fingers and place a clip on it.

I am still breathing through the pain from the first clip, so I have no idea how this is going to go. As soon as the second clip bites my nipple, I arch my back and moan. Yes, it is painful, but it is also incredible. The pulsing. The nerve endings. My clit. Oh, God. An involuntary shudder goes through my whole body. Another wave hits me, and I thrust my breasts out as if to dislodge the clips. They don't move, which makes me feel vulnerable but sexy as hell at the same time.

MISTRESS_CIARA: How are you feeling, pet?

CRYSTAL_TOY: Incredible. The pain –

I groan before finishing the message.

CRYSTAL_TOY: It's going right to my clit. i'm breathing hard, Mistress.

MISTRESS_CIARA: And who gave you that pain?

CRYSTAL_TOY: You did, Mistress. You did. Thank You for punishing me.

MISTRESS_CIARA: We're not done. Go get a chair with no arms."

I stand up, still breathing heavy, and make my way to the kitchen. I have a small table there shoved against the wall with two clean but beat-up thrift store chairs with no arms. As I pick up one of the chairs, I accidentally brush the clip attached to my right nipple. This sends a glorious wave of pain through me. My pussy clenches as if going into orgasm. I will it to slow down as I walk the chair back to my computer.

CRYSTAL_TOY: Chair acquired, Mistress.

MISTRESS_CIARA: I'm sitting down in the chair with the longest of the wooden spoons. Drape yourself over My lap, slave.

I frown. I called me a slave again. I like being her pet, not her slave. But I do as I am told and put my belly on the chair and let my weight fall naturally over the seat. After a couple of adjustments, I am reasonably well balanced. My breasts hang over the edge, pointing toward the ground. I feel vulnerable. Probably more vulnerable than I've ever felt. I had the foresight to put my detached keyboard on the chair so that I can reach it. The wooden spoons lay next to it.

CRYSTAL_TOY: Done, Mistress.

MISTRESS_CIARA: And why are you being punished?

CRYSTAL_TOY: Because i disrespected You, my Mistress.

MISTRESS_CIARA: Take the spoon and whack it into your other hand. Pop it. Yes, that's it.

I do as she requests, and it stings the palm of my left hand.

MISTRESS_CIARA: Harder now. I said harder. you can take more. When you inhale sharply, then that's the force I'm going to use on your ass cheeks.

After about five tentative smacks, I find myself inhaling sharply.

CRYSTAL_TOY: Yes, Mistress. i'm ready for Your punishment.

MISTRESS_CIARA: You deserve this, slave, for Your blatant disrespect.

CRYSTAL_TOY: Yes, Ma'am.

I wait for her instructions. This is incredibly embarrassing, knowing that I am about to hit myself with a wooden spoon. I would die a thousand deaths if anyone saw me. It's embarrassing enough knowing this woman from Columbus knows what I'm doing.

I breathe in, and a jolt of pain shoots from my clamped nipples straight down to my southern region. Oh, God, it hurts so deliciously.

MISTRESS_CIARA: Five quick whacks on your right ass cheek to start. I will not, under any circumstances, hit you in the kidney area or the tailbone. your safety is important, pet. Now, make sure to get the meat. Let Me know when this is done.

I take the longest of the wooden spoons and bend my elbow and reach from behind. I flick my wrist softly so that I can gauge the landing site. I hit the middle of one cheek perfectly, and even that first test swing stings a little. How am I going to handle full force swings? And five of them. I take another deep breath and brace myself by placing my left hand flat on the floor for balance. With my right hand, I flick my wrist and whack my ass with all I've got. The pain is sudden and sharp. It hurts. I don't allow myself to think too much about the pain and hit myself again, trying to find a slightly different spot. Three more whacks after that, and I am done. The pain radiates through my core and then settles in my pussy and my clit.

"Oh, my God," I say to my apartment. I breathe out through the pain as it continues to pulse and radiate through me.

MISTRESS_CIARA: Five more, slave. On the other cheek.

CRYSTAL_TOY: Yes, Ma'am. Hurts so good.

MISTRESS_CIARA: Do it.

Five more whacks send the same pain, but the pleasure is spreading as well.

CRYSTAL_TOY: Done.

MISTRESS_CIARA: Five more on each cheek. Go.

Impossibly, I am looking forward to these next five. My wrist snaps five times, and I exhale on each one, welcoming the pain, bringing it into myself instead of fighting it. I switch hands. My left hand and wrist are not as adept as my right, I find.

CRYSTAL_TOY: Ohhhh.

I breathe through the heady sensations.

CRYSTAL_TOY: Done.

MISTRESS_CIARA: There were three transgressions. you have five more on each side. This time hit the upper part of each leg. Do *not* hit your sensitive genital area, slave. The goal is punishment, not disfigurement.

I do as commanded and breath hard as my pussy pulses slowly as if wanting to go into pre-orgasm. This is so unexpected. I can't believe pain is causing this.

MISTRESS_CIARA: How wet are you now, My pet?

I type furiously.

CRYSTAL_TOY: Mistress, i am breathing hard. i am impossibly wet. i need to cum.

CRYSTAL_TOY: Please, Mistress, let me cum. i am pulsing. i am dying.

MISTRESS_CIARA: Cum for Me, pet. Cum all over My lap. Let Me feel your wetness on the chair. Let me see your visual apology for disrespecting your Mistress. Cum, pet, cum.

She doesn't have to tell me twice. My hands are on my pussy in seconds. Still draped over the chair, two fingers from my left hand fly inside my folds while my right hand attacks my clit. My moan is low in timbre and long. Within seconds I am cumming. Tremors rock my body from the center of my sex. I continue to rub and thrust until every ounce of my energy is spent. My body is heavy as I lose all awareness of the rest of my world. Pulse after pulse takes my breath away.

When I finally regain my composure, I type a message.

CRYSTAL_TOY: Holy fucking God! Mistress, that was incredible. OMG.

MISTRESS_CIARA: I felt the tremors here in Columbus, pet. Big smile.

MISTRESS_CIARA: Slide three fingers through your wetness and then lick them. Suck them. I want to know how you taste today.

I do as I am told and am incredibly surprised.

CRYSTAL_TOY: i taste good, Mistress.

MISTRESS_CIARA: As I knew you would.

MISTRESS_CIARA: I have to go now. But I am looking forward to meeting my sweet-tasting pet in less than two weeks.

CRYSTAL_TOY: Yes, Ma'am.

I am surprised at my automatic response. As soon as I hit the enter key, I cringe. What happened to my resolve *not* to go to Columbus? To *not* let her see my face? To *not* meet her? As I say my goodnights to her, I am as confused as ever.

Chapter Eight

Good Girl

The construction alone on I-71 North is enough to jangle my nerves, but the closer I get to Columbus, the shakier my nerves make me. It is the Wednesday before Thanksgiving, and I've left plenty of time to drive the approximately hour and three-quarters from Cincy. My body is in complete turmoil. I am squirming with nerves, but I am also so wet with excitement that I am almost uncomfortable. I follow the Black Oak Restaurant's GPS directions, where I am meeting her at seven o'clock. I am early. It's only six-thirty. If the construction hadn't slowed me down, I would have been here at six o'clock or sooner.

The Black Oak is a nice-looking place. The parking area is tree-lined and in the center is a massive oak. It must be a *black* oak, I reason, hence the name of the restaurant. There are lights tastefully hanging from the lowest branches making the tree a beautiful focal point. The building itself reminds me of the one time I went to New Orleans. The faux second story of the restaurant has wrought-iron railings and ornate columns. Mistress Ciara has picked a classy restaurant. That must mean *she* is classy. But what am I? Probably whatever the complete opposite of classy is. I drive to the far edge of the lot, where I can watch the front entrance for a while. I know what she looks like from her pictures on *Kinks but* seeing a person in the flesh may be quite different.

I leave the car running for the heater but turn the headlights off. I text Miss Olga that I arrived at the restaurant and send her a picture of the lit-up tree. She texts me back immediately, thanking me for letting her know that I got there. She also reminds me to have fun. I resist commenting back to her. This may start a conversation, and I can't really focus on that right now. I still have to message Lisa. She and I have become quite friendly in the two weeks since we start chatting on *Kinks*.

CRYSTAL_TOY: Made it. I'm early. The place looks classy and swanky. I may be underdressed.

RACHELS_TOY: Glad you made it. Believe me when I say that tonight is about Mistress Ciara and your ability to make her feel like a queen. From the pictures you sent me of your outfit, honey, you are smoking hot and will be fine.

The outfit she's referring to is a recent purchase just for this occasion. I bought a soft but tight long-sleeved form-fitting sweater over a push 'em up and out bra. I was surprised at how much the cerulean blue sweater brought out the blue in my eyes. I also have on a black blazer and a pair of camel-colored slacks to complete the outfit. Amazingly my cowlick is behaving, too. I even pulled out my long dangly earrings that Lisa thought would look lovely with my short hair. Of course, Lisa has never seen my short hair or face, but she got the general idea.

I blush at her assessment.

CRYSTAL_TOY: Thanks. I'm nervous.

RACHELS_TOY: Of course, you are. You wouldn't be human if you weren't. Even *I'm* nervous for you. Okay, I am not going to keep you, dear. Please send me a message at 8 pm and then when you're headed home. If you're staying overnight, let me know. We'll set up a time for you to text me in the morning. Okay?

I laugh. She is becoming kind of a mother hen.

CRYSTAL_TOY: Yes, okay. Okay to all of that.

RACHELS_TOY: LOL. I sure can be bossy, can't I? Rachel tells me that all the time.

CRYSTAL_TOY: Thank you, dear friend.

RACHELS_TOY: And afterward? I want details, details, details.

CRYSTAL_TOY: Sigh. Okay. Will do. Bye for now.

RACHELS_TOY: Bye and good luck!

I close the app and take a deep breath. I have had my eye on the front door the entire time but see no sign of my Mistress. I wait a few more minutes and then decide that I should head inside. Maybe she's already in there waiting for me, and I already know how much she hates to wait.

When I walk in the door, the atmosphere blows me away. From the stone fireplace to the white tablecloths to the candles, the place is a romantic paradise. It is dimly lit and creates just the right cozy feel.

A cute early-twenties-something receptionist showing enough cleavage to make me blush ushers me to a coat check room and then asks if I have a reservation. When I tell her that I am waiting for a friend, I almost say, "I am meeting Mistress Ciara," but catch myself in time and say, "I am meeting my friend, Ciara."

"Ahh," the young receptionist says. "And you are Crystal?"

"Yes." I am surprised that she knows my name.

"Miss Ciara is not yet here, but her table is ready. Follow me."

I have no choice but to follow the cute young thing to a back-corner booth. Good, this will give us some privacy. It isn't completely isolated, but we'll be able to talk freely here. The white tablecloth is oversized and hangs low. As I slide into the booth, I am careful not to pull the cloth with me and destroy the beautiful place settings.

"Make yourself comfortable," the receptionist says and then adds, "Your drink will be here in a moment."

"My drink? I didn't order –" I stop mid-sentence when she simply smiles and walks away. *Okay, that's just weird.* Within moments, a cute blonde late-twenties-something waiter approaches with a glass of wine on a tray. His white shirt, black pants, and white apron suit him. He sets the glass down in front of me.

"Mmm," he says to me, "you are so cute. I'm so glad she's going back to women for a while," he says as if this is supposed to make me feel good.

I am not sure what to say to him, so I just smile.

"Okay, so first of all, Mistress is very kind, but do *not* cross her. The best way to cross her is to get drunk, so I recommend you don't go beyond two glasses." He gestures toward the wine. "Sip slowly."

I am taken aback by him telling me how to manage myself and feel my brow furrow. And, I realize, he referred to her as 'Mistress.' He knows.

"You'll be fine if you let Mistress run the show, okay?"

I nod and decide that perhaps I should speak at some point. "Okay. Anything else?"

"Oh, yes. She always pays for women, but you should offer to pay first. When she refuses, ask if you can at least pay for the tip. She may take you up on that. Keep in mind that she'll ask you to pay upwards of 30%."

"Thirty?"

"We take care of her, so she takes care of us." He smiles, and the smile reaches his eyes. "Now, I will be your waiter, and I will help you every step of the way. Let her steer the conversation, but you probably already know this. What else, what else?" He slowly taps his index finger on his chin and then gasps. "Oh, my God, I can't believe I almost forgot. Stand when she

95

arrives. And, whatever you do, don't sit until she is fully seated. It shows that you respect her. And that, my dear, will take you very far. Let's see. What else. Eat at her pace. Don't wolf your food, but definitely eat. She will not be pleased if you don't eat. Small bites, though, because you do *not* want to have to talk with your mouth full. Oh, and let her talk to me and the other wait staff. You pretty things are to be seen and not heard." He laughs and then touches me on the arm. "Honey, you'll be okay. You're cute, and you have the most crystalline blue eyes I've ever seen."

Before I can respond, he whips his head around and says excitedly, "She's here. She's here."

I take a deep breath as I slowly turn toward the front entrance. I stand up as instructed. Oh, my God. She is beautiful. She looks even better than her photographs on *Kinks*. A gold knit dress clings to her like a second skin. The color accentuates her dark skin perfectly. Her dark hair is straight and just barely reaches her shoulders. Her lipstick is the most perfectly applied deep pink and makes her lips lush and full. The receptionist looks a little flustered, as if she is in the presence of royalty. And judging by the way most of the eyes in the restaurant are on my Mistress, she just might be some kind of celebrity. I am suddenly feeling very territorial about her.

"Isn't she perfect?" the waiter says with awe.

"Yes," is all I can say. I am overwhelmed. And then I can't help but wonder why the fuck she's having dinner with the likes of *me*? My personal waiter leaves my side, and I feel completely abandoned. I swallow down my nerves as I wait for her arrival at the table.

She moves easily through the restaurant, greeting wait staff and bartenders by name. It is a full ten minutes before she arrives at the table alongside the receptionist.

"Your drink will be here shortly, Miss," the receptionist says. "Is there anything else I can do for you?"

"No, Mandy," Mistress Ciara says. "You go on now." And just like that, the receptionist is dismissed.

I stand up straight as my Mistress slowly turns to face me. Blood rushing to my cheeks. I can't help it. She is majestic.

"Crystal," Mistress Ciara says.

"Yes, Ma'am," I say. "It's so nice to meet you." I make no move to embrace her or take her hand. *She* is in charge. She will lead. I will follow.

"You are a beautiful woman, Crystal," she says and raises one approving eyebrow. "Please. Sit." She gestures toward my side of the booth.

"After you, Ma'am," I say smoothly. She is a tall woman. Several inches taller than I am, but then again, she's wearing heels.

The smile on her face grows. She nods and then takes her seat. Once she is settled, I sit, being mindful not to pull at the oddly long tablecloth. I only have eyes for her, but I can feel the entire restaurant looking in our direction. I take a slow breath, trying to calm my nerves and block out the rest of the world.

I smile as I wait for her to speak.

"How was your trip here?" She asks me with a smile. "Not too much Thanksgiving traffic, I hope."

"Not too much, Ma'am. A bit of construction slowed me down, but I allowed for that."

The smile she gives me lights up my entire core. "Good thinking, pet."

The blond waiter gently interrupts us by bringing a glass of red wine to the table. He sets it in front of Mistress Ciara and hesitates for a moment. She very subtly waves her hand dismissively. He backs away with a nod and leaves.

"Pet," she addresses me, "it's okay to call me Mistress. The staff knows who you are."

My eyes must have gotten wide because she adds, "Not your name or what you do. Just that you're my new submissive. They're all curious. They all want to *be* you. Enjoy it."

"Yes, Ma'am." I am about to go silent but then blurt out, "May I say something, Mistress?"

"Of course, pet. Please do."

"Mistress, you are positively the most beautiful woman I have ever seen." I blow out a breath of air.

She laughs and says, "Thank you, pet. You're a good girl."

Her words go straight to my southern region, and I try not to hyperventilate.

"So, tell me about yourself, pet." She smiles at me and adds, "No pressure. Whatever you can share." She takes a sip from her wine glass, so I do, too. Maybe the alcohol will calm my nerves.

"I, uh, …" I'm not sure what to tell her. "I am four months out of a four-year relationship, and uh …" Just then, my eyes do the unthinkable. They drift down to her cleavage, where her ample breasts are hugged so deliciously by the gold knit fabric.

Mistress Ciara chuckles. "Do you like what you see?"

I slam my eyes shut and groan. My face turns molten hot. "I'm sorry, Mistress. Yes, yes, I adore what I see. I'm sorry for being so outlandishly rude."

"It's not rude. I like being appreciated by my pets." She looks down at my breasts and says, "It looks like I'm having a visual effect on you, dear."

At first, I don't know what she's talking about, so I follow her gaze and realize that both of my nipples are standing up hard and firm and tenting my tight sweater. I am mortified. "Yes, Ma'am," I choke out. "You have that effect on me."

"Hmm," is all she says. "So, you're single then."

"Yes, Ma'am."

"Do you like being single?"

I laugh. "If it means not being in my old relationship, then yes."

She chuckles again, and I'm cheering inside that I'm able to make her smile. "Let's go for a more fun topic. Favorite cartoon character?"

"Winnie the Pooh," I blurt without hesitation. Oh, God. What am I? Seven?

"That was fast."

I don't dare tell her that I sleep with a Winnie the Pooh stuffie. That began when Jen started pulling away from me, and I couldn't cuddle her at night anymore. "I have always adored the Winster. Since I was a kid."

She smiles again. It's a knowing smile that I can't make sense of.

"How about you, Mistress? Do you have a favorite?"

"No, I'm not much into that."

Now I feel like an idiot. Thank God I see the blond waiter making his way over. But it is not in my destiny for him to save me right now because, with the slightest flick of the fingers on her right hand, Mistress Ciara sends him away before he even gets close.

She leans close to me as if she is going to whisper something. I lean close, as well.

"Are you wet, my pet?"

A spike of lust shoots through me at her words. "Yes," I choke out with an unsteady voice.

"Spread your legs wide."

My eyes grow wide, but I do as I'm told. Within seconds her bare foot slides up my inner thigh. My jaw drops open at her boldness.

She says, "Look at me." I do. "Whose cunt is this?" She asks this as her big toe presses against my sex.

I swallow hard, and before I can answer, her eyes sharpen and tell me that I must give the right answer. With a shaking voice, I say, "Yours." I swallow hard again. "Yours, Mistress." I now understand the reason for the extra-long tablecloth. No one in the restaurant can see what she is doing to me under the table.

"Good answer, pet. That's right. This cunt is mine." The ball of her foot has now found my center, and her toes repeatedly curl as they massage my outer lips.

"Oh, God," I murmur as her foot moves, and her toes find my clit. I shudder. I can't help it. I don't dare turn my head to see if anyone is watching. I put a hand up as inconspicuously so I can hide my face.

"So responsive to my touch," she says. "A bit of a slut, aren't you? A big whore? Coming to Columbus to open your legs for me? In public?" She raises an eyebrow. Oh, God, she's waiting for a response.

"Yes," is all I say.

Her toes stop moving, and she raises her eyebrow again.

"Yes, Mistress," I quickly amend. "I am. I'm a big whore. I'm *your* whore." Oh, God. What am I saying to this woman I just met?

Her toes start moving again, and she increases the pressure. I am reaching the point of no return. "Mistress –" I slam my eyes shut as a pre-orgasmic pulse hits me. "You … I'm … Oh, God. Oh, God." I grip the edge of the table as my orgasm slams into me. Wave after wave hits my body. My muscles spasm involuntarily as I cum. I try my best to hide my state, but I know she knows.

"Look at me, pet."

My eyes have rolled themselves back up into my head, and they are still there when I open them. It takes great effort to force them forward to look at and focus on my Mistress.

"Such a good whore," she says quietly. I detect pride in her voice.

"Thank you, Mistress," I say breathlessly and then smile. I know she can see my labored breathing.

Her foot slows down its movements. "Your panties are soaked. I can feel it."

"Yes," I say succinctly as the pulses keep coming, although more slowly.

"I will need more proof." She reaches into her purse and pulls out a small dark bag. She slides it toward me. "Go to the ladies' room. Take off your panties and make sure they are good and soaked with your juices. Put them in this bag."

I moan as another pulse hits me right in my center. Oh, God, what her words do to me. "Yes, Mistress." I breathe out a long slow breath. I can't believe I have to get up and walk right now. And, why, oh why did I wear light-colored pants? I take the bag and disassociate somewhat as I head toward the restroom. Who am I? I wonder this as I open the door to the blessedly empty room. I head to the farthest stall, go in, and then stand with my back against the closed door for a moment. Did I, a well-regarded professor of mathematics, just have public sex in a bustling restaurant? I put a hand up as if to ward off the thought. I close my eyes and take a deep breath. As I let it out slowly, I try not to melt down. To distract myself, I pull out my phone and send a quick message to Lisa, telling her that I am fine. She answers back that she is relieved and that I should "have a good time."

Instead of dealing with what I've done out there in the restaurant with a woman I just met, I decide to process it later. Much later. In the meanwhile, I have a task to do for my Mistress.

Once the deed is done and I've cleaned up as best I can, I discretely carry the bag back to the table. I am surprised to see that our table has been served with foods of all kinds.

"Just in time, my pet," Mistress Ciara says jovially. "A smorgasbord for us. I always order a variety, so I'm sure there's something here you would like."

"Thank you, Mistress," I say as I sit down. "Everything looks wonderful." There is a large Caesar salad, a beef dish of some kind, lasagna, asparagus, a small cheese pizza, and a host of other dishes. She reaches her hand across the table, palm up. I place the bag in it, and she beams at me in a lecherous way. I swallow hard. Oh, my God. Who am I?

She puts the bag away in her purse and then gestures toward the food. "Take whatever you like, pet. You are being rewarded. You did well. Very well."

"Thank you," I whisper. My face flushes, but this time with pride. "I can't help it, being so near you, Mistress." It may sound like I'm blowing smoke, but I'm not. I'm sincere. This time I have appealed right to her ego, and she smiles a smug and satisfied smile. Yes, Mistress, you have me. You've snagged me hook, line, and sinker.

"And do you know how else I reward my pets?" She says, spooning what looks like beef stroganoff onto her plate.

When she is finished, I do the same. "No, Mistress. How do you reward your pets?"

"By taking them home."

My eyes grow wide. I knew there was a possibility of this, but now that it might be real. And I am petrified.

"But not tonight," Mistress Ciara adds coolly. "Tomorrow is Thanksgiving, and I have family plans. Will you be able to come back up on Friday? Stay through Sunday?"

My danger nerves should have paralyzed me, but instead, a surge of lust races through me. I am overwhelmed with desire that I cannot think straight. What would Lisa tell me to do right now? Should I say that I need to think it over? That I will get back to her tomorrow? That makes sense. My head and body will be a lot cooler, and I will be able to think better.

Maybe I can excuse myself and go back to the restroom to message Lisa. She'll ask me the same question she asked me a while ago. "Do you want to go?" My answer back then was yes. I look up at my Mistress and swallow hard. My mouth had become dry all of a sudden. As I look at her questioning face, I realize that yes, yes, I do want to go home with her. I want to see where she lives and how she lives. I want to know everything about her. And, most importantly, I want her to touch me with more than just her foot.

I swallow a second time and look her directly in the eye as my alter-ego takes over. I close my mouth and grin. Decision made.

She chuckles and says, "Is that a yes, pet?"

I nod once. "Yes, Mistress." Outside I look calm. I hope I do, anyway. But inside, I am freaking out. What am I doing? Oh, my God. Who the fuck am I?

She doesn't respond for a while as she studies my face. Slowly, one eyebrow raises, and she takes a slow, satisfied breath. "Good girl. Good, good girl."

Chapter Nine

White Slave Girl

It is Friday evening, and I ring the doorbell to her townhouse at fifteen seconds past seven o'clock. She opens the door, and there she is, the woman I call Mistress.

"Come in, Bernadette," she says and moves to one side to let me in. She is so fucking beautiful. I can't breathe. I don't know what she sees in me, a soft butch with a bad haircut. Her dark skin is smooth, and her blouse hugs her curves superbly—her breasts. Oh, God, I can't look, or I will lose it where I stand. I'm already wet, and I've been here for ten seconds.

She closes the door behind me and then takes my car keys and the meager bag I packed for my weekend stay. There isn't much in it; she said I wouldn't need clothes. I blow out a sigh as she puts my bag on a shelf and then stands in front of me. "Strip."

"Now?" I cringe at my reaction. Seriously? That is the first thing I say to her?

Her eyes narrow as she leans closer. "Now, *what*?" she asks evenly.

I wrack my brain. I don't understand what she wants, but then something snaps into clear focus, and I inhale sharply. Fuck! I'm in trouble within the first minute. "Now, *Mistress*?" Even I hear the meekness in my voice.

"Better, pet. No more slip-ups." She takes a small step back and says, "I won't tell you again."

With shaking hands, I take off my jacket and then unbutton my shirt. Oh, fuck. What have I gotten myself into? Her eyes never leave me as I take

103

off my clothes. I feel myself blushing all over, especially when it's time to pull down my panties. This is the first time she is seeing me naked in person. My white skin turns pink under her gaze betraying my nerves. A small smirk creeps up her face. She likes that I am uncomfortable.

I had a weak moment during our chat the night before, and I told her my real first name. She thanked me for trusting her and said she would not reveal it to anyone. I was not to worry, she said. Another thing she said to me last night was that she was looking for a white female slave. And she hoped that would be me. For some reason, I didn't tell her that I didn't want to be anyone's slave because maybe I do. I like how she sometimes calls me her pet and sometimes calls me her slave. She even calls me a whore and a slut, and to my amazement, I find that I *want* to be called these things. I'm still not sure why. She is my strong black Domme, my Mistress, and I am her submissive. Maybe her white slave. I don't know what that means, though. I hope she will tell me before the weekend is over. Maybe I will get up the nerve to ask.

"Kneel," she commands once all my clothes are neatly folded and placed on an empty shelf. She points, and I see a pillow on the floor near a recliner.

My heart smiles when I see that she remembered about my destroyed knees from years of playing softball. I kneel. She approaches me with something in her hand. My heart almost stops. It is a leather collar. And it's red. So that's why she asked me what my favorite color was during dinner on Wednesday. I don't move an inch as she stands behind me and fastens it around my neck. When she finishes, she moves in front of me and cups my chin firmly. "Be a good girl, now, and stay here. Keep your eyes down." She pulls my head down by my chin.

I look down at my hands, resting on my naked thighs. My breasts are like two white ghosts lying on my chest. They rise and fall quickly; my breathing is shallow. I am one part excited, and one part petrified. I will be okay, though. I have my safety messages set up for the entire weekend, and I've already let both Miss Olga and Lisa know that I arrived here in one piece. I even have secret words that I'm to use every time I message Lisa. That was her idea. Now all I have to do is hope that I'll still be in one piece when it's time to leave on Sunday.

Mistress Ciara moves away from me, and I hear her walking up the stairs. I look up. I should not have. She races back to me and forces my head down with a firm push of her hand.

"I'm sorry, Mistress. I'm sorry." Shit, that's twice now that I've fucked up.

I hear her go up the steps again, and I keep my eyes down as if the oxygen I breathe depends on it. After a while, I hear her come back down. She stands in front of me, and I see the hem of a silk robe. I want to look up at her so badly. Her robe opens, but all I can see are her dark shapely calves. She leans down and snaps a leash onto my collar. I blow out a shaky sigh.

"Look up, pet," she commands softly.

I do, and right before me is her clean-shaven pussy. I sigh. It's perfect. I swallow hard. It's uber-obvious what's next. I look up higher to see her face, my neck craning uncomfortably. Her closed-lipped smile is reassuring. Sort of. She looks like she's trying to decide the many ways she is going to wreck me this weekend.

"You know what to do." She tugs on the leash, pulling me even closer. She wraps her hands in my short blonde hair and pulls me to her pussy. Her scent is divine. I am at the altar. "Lick me, pet. Lick and worship your black Mistress's pussy as a white slave girl should." She presses my face into her warm wet folds. She has me pressed so hard into her that I can only lick a short distance. "Lick your first real black pussy." I haven't licked anyone's pussy in years, but it's like riding a bicycle, and I now remember how much I love giving girl-head.

I give her short strokes and then longer ones when she relaxes the pressure on the back of my head. "That's a good girl. Keep licking." I swirl my tongue around her outer lips and then her clit. It is so engorged it's like a little penis sticking up for me to kiss, and I do. I then catch it in my lips and suck gently. I run the hard tip of my tongue over the top. Her quick exhale tells me that she is pleased. She grinds her hips into my face and says, "Ah, Bernadette, now you will finally feel fulfilled as you learn how to worship Mistress Ciara's pussy like the dirty little whore that you are."

A wave of pure adrenaline shoots through me at her words, and my pussy clenches. I moan into her folds. I am so fucking wet that my juices are dripping down the inside of my thighs. And she hasn't even touched me.

She grinds against my face. I hang on, offering my lips, my tongue, my chin, my nose. Her juices coat my face. I thrust inside her as deep as my tongue will go and alternate thrusting with swirling her clit. After a while, she holds me still on her clit. "Lick it, slave. Lick it." Her breathing gets heavy, and she heaves against me. She's coming. She's coming right on my face. I feel her pussy spasm against my tongue. I keep licking. It has become my only purpose in life. Her breathing finally slows, and she pushes me away, one hand still wrapped in my hair. I lean back slightly, my ass resting on my heels. She doesn't say or do anything for several long moments. She is basking in the afterglow. I want desperately to look up at her, but I am not allowed.

Finally, she tousles my hair and sighs. "You did well, pet. Very well."

I almost cry at how much I wanted to hear those words from her. My Mistress is pleased with me. That's all I want.

"Look up."

I almost choke when I see her holding the biggest black dildo I have ever seen.

"It's time for you and BBC to get acquainted." She presses the tip against my lips. "Kiss her, Bernadette. Kiss my big black cock. Let her know how much you want her inside your body."

I kiss the black silicone head.

She pushes the tip inside my mouth. She doesn't push it in far, thank God. I've put my own dildo in my mouth, but I've never had a partner do it. It's odd not being in control of something like that. I'm sure Mistress Ciara loves being in control of what she does to me, to my body.

She pushes in a little further. "Use your tongue, Bernadette. Feel the veins along her shaft." I lick the dildo and am amazed at how lifelike it is, not that I've ever had a dick in my mouth. She pulls it out until only the head remains. "Lick her head again, pet. Show her some love." As I'm licking the head, she slowly pushes the dildo in my mouth and then pulls it back out. "Keep your tongue out of the way and watch those teeth." She thrusts in and out again, and I realize she is teaching me how to suck her BBC. She understands that I have had no experience with this kind of thing.

I moan involuntarily as she fucks my mouth.

"You like this, you little white whore, don't you?" She asks. I can hear the smugness in her voice.

"Mm-hmm," is all I can say. I have a dildo in my mouth. She pushes the dildo in a little farther and increases the distance until she bumps up against the back of my throat.

"Don't you gag, whore," she commands. "Don't you gag." Miraculously, I don't, but I realize that I must relax my jaw and throat, or I *will* gag. "It's all in the breath," she says. "Find the rhythm. Breathe around it and in time with BBC's thrusts." She places one hand on the back of my head and wraps her fingers in my hair. She pulls my head up slightly. It doesn't hurt, but it's her way of letting me know she's in charge and in control.

Her strokes quicken, and I find that I am hanging in there just fine. Who knew I'd be good at sucking dick? I almost laugh at the thought but can't. I need to focus on breathing. Three big final thrusts each hit the back of my throat, and this time I do gag. She pulls her BBC out of my mouth and pushes my head away as if disgusted with me. I feel as if I have failed her.

"You have to do better, Bernadette. I told you last night about the Mistresses joining us tomorrow. They're coming over at my request to help me evaluate your slave potential. They have my permission to have their way with you. And Nikki is definitely going to fuck your mouth like this. You cannot embarrass me in front of the other Dommes when they are here, slave." She grabs my chin and forces my head back. "Is that understood?"

I nod as well as I can with my chin in her hand. "May we try again, Mistress?" I can't believe I'm asking for another go at the dildo.

"Of course, dear pet. I like your attitude." She presents the head at my lips again, and I kiss it. She beams. "Good girl." This time I stay focused. Without warning, she pushes in fast and hard and hits the back of my throat. I was ready for it this time and, by some miracle, don't gag. She varies her thrusts, and I stay with her. I moan again as I picture her BBC as part of her actual body and that she feels every lick and stroke.

"Suck a little now. Make it harder for me to pull BBC out of your slut mouth." After a couple of tries, I find just the right amount of suction to please her. "Nikki will be expecting you to know how to do this tomorrow."

"Mm-hmm," I say when she thrusts in and out again. Her hand is back in my hair, and I know what that means. I am ready. This time it wasn't three rams, it was five, and I hang on as her BBC pummels my throat. She pulls out abruptly, and I gasp for breath.

"Kiss her, pet. Let her know how grateful you are." I kiss her BBC and am secretly pleased with myself. I hope I do her proud when Mistress Nikki is here tomorrow.

She places her BBC down on her recliner chair and opens her robe. "You've made me wet again, pet. Lick me. I want to cum all over your white whore face again."

Involuntarily, I lick my lips to get ready to service my Mistress again. She chuckles at this as she pulls me closer to her sex. "Make me cum, slave. This is your life's goal. To please me."

Her words send another jolt of lust rocketing through me, and I feel myself gush. I shiver – partly from the coolness of the temperature in her townhouse and partly from my incredibly turned-on state.

As I lick my Mistress, I pay attention and learn what turns her on and what makes her still my head when I've hit the perfect spot. As I discover these things, I can't help but wonder how many other lips and tongues have performed this same service for her. I can't think about that now, though. What I do think is that *I* am the one who is here now. *I* am the one she calls pet and slave and whore and slut. *I* am Mistress Ciara's slave, her white slave girl. Me, not them!

Chapter Ten

Two Out of Three

My Mistress sucks air through her teeth slowly. She sighs her pleasure and then basks in the afterglow while I wait on my knees in front of her. I am positively beaming to have satisfied her twice now. My entire being yearns for her to tell me that I'm a good girl or say that I did well. But that doesn't happen.

Instead, my Mistress tugs on my leash and says, "Stand, slave." I stand and have no choice but to follow where she pulls me. She brings me into the kitchen and flicks a switch—bright light bursts into the room. My nakedness seems harsh in this light. I lick my lips. I am suddenly thirsty. I taste the sweetness of her cum all over them. My face is still damp from licking her in the living room. I like it; she has marked me. I know it's not permanent, but it is from her.

"Water?" she asks. I nod. "Get your bowl." She gestures to a bowl on the kitchen table.

"Really, Mistress? For me?" She nods. "Thank you." I hurry over and retrieve what is apparently going to be my water bowl. It's a dog bowl, but it's mine. She got it for me. I know this because it has little Winnie the Poohs all the way around it. I am a grown woman in her early thirties, but I don't care. She got it for me. "Thank you, Mistress. I love it." I hold it to my chest. The metal is cold against my bare breasts.

"Fill it from the water cooler and then put it in that elevated stand," she commands gently.

I do as I'm told, and then she pushes me down to a squat in front of the bowl. My old softball knees protest a little, but they hold. She stands beside me. I love the contrast between us – her black skin and my white. She commands me to drink, and I have, like, zero seconds to figure out how. This reminds me of bobbing for apples as a kid. I always choked when my nose went into the water. I lean over. My ass sticks up in the air as I do so. I try hard not to make a fool of myself in front of my Mistress as I figure out how to drink without choking. My lips go in first, and the tip of my nose follows. As long as I keep my nostrils out of the water, I can suck up a large amount. I take a huge sip and then another and another. I didn't realize how thirsty I was. Part of me, the wary part, is expecting my Mistress to push my head in the water bowl, but even though my Mistress is strict, I don't think she's mean. I'm not sure yet, because this is our first "in real life" weekend together instead of our many virtual meetings on *Kinks*. I lean forward to take a few more sips.

A warm hand strokes my ass. "Such a glaring white slave-girl ass." Besides grabbing my chin and lacing her fingers in my hair, this is the first time she's touched me. I am already beyond excited, and I'm sure she can smell my muskiness from there. She kneads my flesh like dough and then gently separates my ass cheeks, exposing me. "BBC is going to like this ass," she says as if picturing the moment. I, for one, am panicking. BBC is a huge dildo. Bigger than I've ever used and bigger than I've ever seen. "Hmm," she muses, her hand is now stroking the backs of my thighs. She must feel how sloppy wet I am. "No, actually," she says pensively, "I think BBC will claim another one of your three holes tonight." Her breathing has gotten a little heavy. My Mistress is excited, which makes my heart soar. "I'm allowed an inspection first, though." Without warning, she thrusts a finger deep into my pussy.

I moan at the intrusion and push back against her. I receive a stinging swat on my ass for my efforts.

"Stay still, slave." Her voice is stern. I don't move while she fucks me with one finger. One finger turns to two, then three. She pushes in slowly and pulls almost all the way out. Then back in. My breathing is not only heavy but ragged. I am so fucking turned on, but I'm not allowed to move. This is agony. My Mistress is wrecking me.

She pulls her fingers out abruptly. I am devastated, but then she flicks my swollen clit. I yelp and clamp my legs together. My clit is standing tall and proud but is extremely sensitive. She knows that, doesn't she? She places her fingers under my nose. "Smell yourself, slave. This is the smell of white cunt. You have a cunt because you are a white slave, but now you only worship black pussy. Do you understand the difference?"

"Yes, Mistress. I understand." I say the words she wants me to say, but I *don't* understand. Does she hate me? Does she hate white women? All white people? I swallow hard. I can ask her. I can open my mouth and have actual words come out of it. People do this all the time. But not me. I can't do it. I can't ever do it.

"Open," she says.

I open my mouth.

She puts her fingers in, and I taste myself. I suck her fingers; I know that's what she wants me to do.

"Suck that white girl cunt juice off my fingers, whore. Hurry with it. BBC is getting impatient." I stuff my fears away and lick my juices off her fingers for all I'm worth as if this is my new career in life. She pulls her fingers out of my mouth and then wipes them on my bare back. I am breathing hard now for two reasons. Because I'm so turned on and, honestly, because I'm a little scared. She knows my safe words. We went over them last night during our chat. Green for go, yellow for pause, red for a full stop. Will she honor them?

She pulls me up by the leash. I stand. "Stay," she says, so I do. She turns the light on over the stove and then flicks off the harsh overhead light. It creates a nice warm glow. She grabs my leash and walks me to the kitchen table. "Bend over," she says. "Put that white ass on display."

I bend as told, and a shot of adrenaline spikes through me. For the love of God and all things natural, how does this woman make me so fucking horny? I have never been this way, ever. It's embarrassing. I don't understand it. I really don't, but I'm not going to question it anymore because it's fucking amazing, and that's why I'm still here and not bolting for the door. My thighs hit the edge of the table; I'm apparently too tall for Mistress Ciara's table, so I shuffle my feet back until my hips press more comfortably against the edge. I hear movement behind me and imagine that my Mistress is putting on the harness I saw on the counter. She's probably attaching BBC to it. I imagine this because I dare not turn around and look, even though I desperately want to.

"Spread your legs, pet." I do as I'm told. "That's a good girl. She's such a good whore, isn't she? She can't wait to offer her cunt to BBC. BBC loves white cunt." She nudges my right leg a little farther away from my left. My groin muscles protest the extra stretch, but I bear it.

She inhales through her teeth. I feel warm hands run up and down my back. She is as excited as I am. The hands push my upper body down firmly on the tabletop. My stomach, breasts, and face are forced down on the smooth surface. I turn my head so I can breathe. "Hold on tight, whore," she says. "BBC is going to take you for a ride."

I reach out and grab both sides of the wide table and hold on for dear life.

My Mistress rubs BBC's tip against my inner thighs. She speaks of BBC likes it's a part of her, but to me, it's a big hunk of silicone that's about to rip me open. Mistress rubs her pride and joy through my slickness and over my clit. I jump; I am almost over-stimulated. I receive another stinging swat on my ass. "Stay still, pet." She slides BBC through my wet cunt lips a few more times until finally presenting the tip to my opening. I hardly breathe. She puts the head in. I sigh. She pulls out, and I feel cheated. She puts the head in again and moves in a little deeper. Then back out. She is teasing me, but then all at once, she plunges to the depths, and I cry out. The sensations are almost overwhelming. My Mistress is taking me for the first time. I have never felt so full. She remains still, allowing my body to adjust to BBC's girth.

"What is your color, pet?"

"Green, my beautiful, generous Mistress," I say through my labored breathing. "My color is very green."

"Excellent." She grips my hips tightly. I am in for a ride, that's for sure. She pulls out slowly and plunges back in. She establishes a slow but steady rhythm, one that I can never create for myself with my own dildos. I'm always too impatient. My clit is burning to be touched, but I don't ask. I know I'll be denied. She plunges in and out; her rhythm is hypnotic. She could keep time for a symphony. Even though she's going slowly, my hips are pushed into the wooden table repeatedly. I will have bruises. "I'm fucking you because I can," she says. "Because I want to." She increases BBC's pace. "And I'll fuck you *anytime* I want to, because you are a slave."

My clit starts sending out early-warning pulses. I am going to cum if she keeps this up. She slams herself into me again and again. I whimper.

I jump when she swats my ass. "I can't hear you, Bernadette. BBC needs to know how much you like her inside you. How much you *need* her."

A wave of lust rushes my body, and I moan involuntarily.

My Mistress swats my ass again. The sting is not fun. "You had no voice in your last relationship, did you, Bernadette?" She knows this because I hinted at it during our conversations last week.

I can't think about that now, though, because with every thrust, my clit pulses. I need release, and I need it soon.

She swats me again. I jump. "Let's hear that voice, Bernadette. Open your mouth and let your passion free."

I had been clenching my teeth but open my mouth and let out a moan that comes from somewhere in my depths.

My Mistress rubs one hand up my back. "That's it, pet. Yes, let that out. It's time for the world to hear Bernadette's voice. Your Mistress wants to hear you sing in ecstasy. Reward BBC for her efforts. Don't disappoint us."

It was a command I wasn't sure I could fulfill.

"Mistress," I manage to get out in between her thrusts. "I want to cum. May I cum? Please let me cum."

She laughs. "That's the longest string of words you've put together since you got here." She laughs again and says, "And, no, you cannot cum right now." She gently swats my ass and adds, "But your Mistress does like the sound of a whore begging." Her hips grind into me. She makes a small sound behind me, which tells me she is also enjoying this but in an entirely different way than I am.

Does she want to hear my voice? Well, here it is. "Mistress, let me cum," I beg for release. "My cunt is pulsing. I can't stop it; it's going to –"

I get another smack on my ass.

"Find a way to hold back, slave." She continues to thrust in and out deeply, bottoming out every time. "BBC is rewarding you for being such a good pussy licker. You need to honor that and hold on a bit longer."

"Yes, Mistress." The friction is divine, but it is also killing me. I close my eyes and try to become one with it.

"In fact," she says with an evil tone, "my pet only cums when Mistress allows it. Understood?"

"Yes, Mistress," I mutter unenthusiastically.

"White pets love their Mistress's BBCs inside them, don't they?"

At this point, I start panting. Her words ignite intense sensations, and I can't answer her. Three sharp blows to my ass almost send me over the edge. "Yes, Mistress," I reply with a pant. I don't even remember what the fucking question was.

I hate both my clit and my cunt for betraying me right now. I'm ready to explode, but I've never been able to cum without a couple of strokes on my clit. I give up the silent command for my body to orgasm on its own, and I clunk my head on the table, defeated. I have no choice but to ride BBC. In and out. In and out. Full and empty. I become one with her rhythm. In and out. I am powerless against it. It's the rocking of a boat, a seesaw, a swing. I go with it. I have no choice. My body twitches as my stomach clenches. Something's happening. I've never felt like this before.

My cunt is spasming around BBC, but it's not an orgasm. I haven't tipped over yet. I know what orgasms feel like. My clit is sending out little pulses, too, but I'm not coming. What is this?

"Feel me grinding into you now, pet. Nice and deep. Do you feel how deep BBC is in your cunt?"

Before I know what's happening, my entire soul gets sucked down to my cunt. I moan at the intense sensation. And then, without warning, my soul shoots outward through every cell of my body as an orgasm rips through me. I am everywhere at once. I realize I've been screaming, but I cannot stop. Pulse after pulse hits me like a freight train making me cry out again and again. I twitch on the tabletop. I can't control it. My Mistress continues to fuck me as my personal earthquake continues. After forever, the aftershocks slow down, and I can almost breathe again.

"Fuck." This is the only word I say.

"Bernadette likes BBC," my Mistress says, stating the obvious. She slows her pace and then comes to a stop, buried in me to the hilt.

"Yes." My breathing is still heavy. Aftershocks wrack my entire body, and I can't help loving BBC and the woman attached to it. I love this fucking kitchen table, too. I chuckle when I think about how scared I was that she hated me because I was white. No woman shows hate that way.

She smacks me on the ass. "I see that smile. Tell me."

I can't tell her what I was really thinking, so all I say is, "Exquisite." And it was.

Still buried in me, she leans over my body and strokes my head. "I think I just heard my pet enjoy her first proper orgasm ever."

I laugh and say, "Ya think?"

She swats my ass again, but this time it isn't playful. I'm beginning to tell the difference. I goofed, and I know it. Sorry, I can't think straight. I just got fucked into oblivion. "Ya think, *Mistress*?"

She swats my ass again and then says, "You will be punished for that disrespect, whore. And you'll also be punished for coming before Mistress told you to."

Tell my body that, I think to myself, but don't dare utter the words out loud. I simply close my eyes and wonder what my punishments will be. Mistress slowly pulls BBC out of my sore and battered cunt. I feel empty when she's gone. My wetness is at monsoon levels. It is running down my thighs.

"Stand." I do. "Turn." I do, and then I melt. My beautiful black Mistress stands in front of me. She did this for me, to me. "Kneel." I fall ungracefully to my knees. They hurt, but I can't help what I'm feeling. I hug her legs, my cheek pressed against her thighs. BBC drips above my head. "Thank you, Mistress. Thank you. That was incredible. I've never had such an –"

"Suck me," she interrupts and pulls my head back by the hair. "Take BBC between your lips now, in your mouth, and thank your Mistress by cleaning her properly." She pushes the head to my lips. I open. I am almost used to this now and wrap my lips around the head to suck my juices off. She pushes it in further. I don't really want to play "blowjob" right now. I simply want to bask in the endorphins created by my mind-blowing orgasm, but I am not in charge here. She is. She knows that sucking silicone dicks is not one of my hard limits, so I take it in and remember the breathing techniques she taught me. Maybe this is one of the things she meant about "pushing boundaries." BBC slides over my tongue and then slides out to my lips. She's fucking my face now. "BBC liked taking two of your holes tonight, slave. Oh, yes, what a joy that third hole will be. It's BBC's favorite."

I gag when BBC hits the back of my throat, but my Mistress just pulls back and hits it again. I gag again. This is not sexy. This sucks. "Relax your throat, pet. Take me in. We're not stopping until you've taken me for an entire minute without gagging."

It's the hardest fucking thing I've ever done in my life. I have a doctorate in mathematics, and that wasn't as hard as this is. I thought I had the gag reflex figured out. Apparently not, and once my gag reflex starts, it's hard to squelch. But I do get control, eventually, and my Mistress finally pulls BBC out of my mouth. I alternately love and hate BBC right now.

"Go get water," Mistress says in a tone that says she's disgusted with me. She points to my bowl. Drinking out of a dog bowl has never sounded so good in all my life.

Chapter Eleven

All of You and More

I wake up swatting at something tickling my earlobe but only end up smacking myself in the head. Someone laughs. "Time to get up, pet. You've got a busy day."

I blink my eyes open and try to focus. Where am I? I inhale sharply when reality comes flooding in. Oh, fuck. That's right. This is my first weekend at my Mistress's townhouse. I sit up and smile at her. The soft morning light from the window truly makes her look like a Goddess or something. She smiles at me, but then last night's events come flooding back, and I am distracted.

I licked this woman to orgasm in her living room. Twice. She came all over my face both times. Oh, God. The kitchen table. She took me with her BBC. I was draped face down over the table. I sigh. Best. Fucking. Orgasm. Ever.

"Pet? Are you still with me?" I refocus and look at her amazing deep brown eyes. My Mistress is so beautiful. Her dark hair and her dark skin are mesmerizing. I feel like I've been drugged. Until last night, I had never been with a black girl.

But she's not just a girl. I reach up to touch her cheek, never quite making contact. "My Mistress." OMG, I just said that out loud—right to her face.

She laughs and says, "You're cute first thing in the morning, pet."

I can't help but smile. Last night she let me sleep in her bedroom. When she pulled me into her room by my leash, I was surprised to see a huge red pet bed. It was big enough for me, a 5' 8" grown woman. She even put in some extra memory foam, so I'd be comfortable. As I sit here trying to wake up, I hug the Winnie the Pooh blanket she bought special just for me. She obviously knows how to pamper the inner pet in me. "Thank you for all of this, Mistress." And just as I say it, I remember. My eyes shoot downward. Crap, I have a punishment coming today because I royally fucked up yesterday.

"Chin up, pet." She reaches for my chin and pulls my head up. "You have fifteen minutes to make my bed and yours and then to shower and shave." She reaches down and cups my already shaved sex. "I want my new pet to make a good impression on the two other Mistresses tonight."

My eyes shoot open wide. I had forgotten.

I must have looked stricken or something because she winks at me and says, "You'll be okay, pet." She grabs my earlobe and pulls me up. I have no choice but to stand.

"Your toiletries are in my bathroom, and I put some new clothes out for you to wear." She reaches behind my neck and unlatches the red leather collar she'd put on me within seconds of my arrival last night. "I'll put your new collar and cuffs on you downstairs." She reaches behind me and kneads one of my ass cheeks. "BBC will be entering her favorite hole today." She sighs as if anticipating some fun times ahead. She swats my ass and says, "Go on, pet. You have fourteen and a half minutes left. My breakfast isn't going to cook itself."

I send two quick messages, one to Miss Olga and one to Lisa, telling them both that I am fine and that I enjoyed myself the night before. Then I make both beds in record time and shower quickly but shave slowly. It would never do to end up wounded in such a precarious spot. I towel off and carefully clean up after myself. My new clothes aren't much in the way of clothes, but at least I'll get to wear something today, unlike yesterday. I pull up the pink boi shorts and love how they fit. I hate that they are pink, and she knows that. It's clear that I am in big trouble if she's making me wear a color that I loathe. The pink matching sports bra goes on next. It's a size too small and makes my breasts squish together, spilling me into a muffin top. Oh, look at that! I have cleavage. Who knew? As a soft butch, I don't usually go for cleavage. Mistress Ciara is so good to me. I can't fuck up today. Especially not in front of the other Mistresses.

"One minute to go, pet," she calls from downstairs.

"Shit, shit, shit," I mutter and, with shaking hands, carefully hang my towel on the empty rack. I do my best not to break an ankle on the stairs and pretty much slide onto my knees in front of her just as she'd begun a ten-second countdown.

"I wasn't sure if you were going to make it." She smirks at me, and I can't help but smile back. She pats my head, and I smile bigger. She runs a hand over my new cleavage and licks her lips. "This pink bra looks good on my pet."

I beam. Even though I'm a teacher and talk every day, my Mistress has quickly discovered that I am not much of a talker in her presence. I'm not sure if she likes it that way or not. "You know why you're wearing pink, don't you?" I nod and look down, ashamed. She knows that it is torture for me to wear such a girly color. She reaches behind me and swats me on the ass. I jump at the sting of it. "I didn't hear you, pet."

"Yes, Mistress. I know why I'm wearing pink today."

"And why is that?"

"Because I disrespected you yesterday, Mistress, by not referring to you as *Mistress* a few times." I sigh and cringe as she pulls a leather collar off the table. It's also pink. Blech.

"What else?"

My eyes are still pointed downward. I look at her feet and wonder if she'll ever let me take her slippers off and massage her feet and calves. Oh, God, I want to touch her so badly. I jump again as she smacks my other ass cheek. I clear my throat and say, "Also, I had an orgasm when you told me not to. I'm sorry, Mistress." I didn't know how to tell her that I tried so hard *not* to cum, but BBC was pounding into me, and she was saying all those dirty things in my ear, and my cunt starting pulsing, and there was not a single thing I could do to stop that seismic blast.

She pushes her chair away from the kitchen table. "Stand up." I bolt to my feet, my old softball knees creaking as I do so. "Let's get these out of the way." She pushes my boi shorts down to my ankles but doesn't take them off. She pats her lap. "Place your worthless self over my lap, slave. Ass up."

I wasn't exactly sure how to position myself, but she's clearly done this before and adjusts my body to fit perfectly. Both my feet and hands reach the floor, so I'm able to keep myself steady and not put too much of my weight on her. I think I know what's coming next. Her hand slaps my right ass cheek, and I yelp at the sting of it. Okay, now I'm sure. I am about to get a spanking.

She hits me without warning. The spot pulses and hurts like a mother. She rubs it gently with her cool hand. My left ass cheek is next. I jump again and involuntarily reach back to guard myself. That's what one does when being assaulted. She grabs my arm and holds it tight.

"We can't have this, now, can we?" my Mistress says, and I feel her lean over to reach something on the table. She places something tight around my wrist. It feels like leather. Oh, shit, she's putting a leather wrist cuff on me. "Give me your other arm." I have no choice but to let my weight fall on her as I bend my other arm behind my back. The second cuff goes on just as tight as the first. And then she links them together somehow. I involuntarily try to separate my wrists. But I can't. She lifts my arms and lets them fall as if showing me that she has control now, that I am powerless. "There, now you won't get in my way."

Before I have a chance to register the fact that my hands are bound, two hard smacks land on my right cheek, followed by two on my left. I grunt throughout the blows. A spanking always seemed so benign in my mind, but this shit hurts.

"Do you have a voice, Bernadette?" my Mistress taunts me.

I grunt again as I try to manage the pain.

Both of her hands slowly wrap around my neck. Adrenaline shoots through me, and I whimper as she tightens her grip. "Do. You. Have. A. Voice?"

"Yes," I squeak out around my closing windpipe.

"Then use it," she says and releases my neck so I can breathe again. She smacks each ass cheek once. This time she doesn't rub me. I can't use my voice at the moment like she wants because I'm focusing too much on breathing and hoping this black woman whose lap I'm draped over isn't a serial killer. "What's your color, pet?"

"Um…" I try to swallow, but my mouth has gone dry. "Um," I stammer again. "It's green," I blurt. "It's green," I say again with more certainty. "But, Mistress, I've never been spanked before."

"Look at that," my Mistress says. "She actually *can* speak!" She said it sarcastically, but I hear the praise in her words, too. She rubs both of my ass cheeks. "That was just a warm-up, my pet. I need you to count now. We're going to thirty. If you mess up, we start over."

She smacks my right cheek. "One," I say. My left. "Two." *Bam, bam, bam.* "Three, four five." She pauses for a moment and smooths my ass. I'm getting used to the sharp sting of her smacks, but something surprising is happening. The sting blooms into a warmth that spreads beyond my ass cheeks through my core to my chest. I hear my breathing get heavy. With my hands clasped behind my back, I am powerless. I don't know when the next smack will be.

Smack on my right. "Six." The sting turns into a tingling warmth that spreads through me. This time it goes right to my cunt, and I feel myself getting excited.

Smack on my left. "Seven." Then *bam, bam, bam.* The sting alternates from my right to my left and back again. I groan and then say, "Seven, eight, nine."

"Aww, little pet," she says. "You didn't make it very far."

"What?" I pant out the words. Getting spanked is fucking incredible. "Mistress?" I know the title is too late, but maybe she won't notice.

"You said seven twice, pet. Now we have to start over." Her tone is one of extreme disappointment.

I want to protest. I know how to fucking count, and I *know* I didn't say the number seven twice. Or did I? I can't think right now. There's too much sensation.

"We're going on a steady rhythm now to thirty. Try to keep up," she says. By some miracle of the gods, I do keep up. And by the time she reaches thirty, my ass and the backs of my legs are burning. And so is my cunt. I am so caught up in sensation that I decide I am just going to have to live on my Mistress's lap for all of eternity. Except that the blood has kind of pooled in my head that's hanging off her lap, and I'm getting light-headed.

Her smooth hands are gently rubbing my body. "Color, pet?" she says softly.

I say, "Mmm."

She laughs. "That's not a color."

"Gree," I say. It's the best I can do. I can't speak. I am in bliss.

"Close enough," she says with another laugh. I feel her lean toward the kitchen table again. "Use your hands to spread your cheeks."

Her words don't register at first. I'm still flying high from my first spanking since leaving childhood. I mean, my ass hurts, and it's pulsing, and I desperately want her to rub my burning skin some more, but that's okay. Somehow, I feel good.

"Cheeks, pet."

Hmm? Did she say cheeks? What cheeks? After forever, it dawns on me what she's asking me to do. I arch my back so that my hands will reach my ass, but I can't spread them since my hands are face up. "Mistress? I can't, uh, my hands are not positioned right."

"Oh, you're right. Let's fix that." She unclasps my wrist cuffs, and then I can reach. I rub my sore cheeks a couple of times for relief and then pull them apart. Something obviously is going to be going into my virgin hole. I've never had a dildo or anything in there, ever.

"That's my good girl," my Mistress says to me. I smile, but it's getting hard to keep my back arched as I hold my upper body up to reach my ass cheeks. "A little investigation," she says and merrily dips two fingers into my sopping cunt. "Well, well. My pet has revealed that she's a pain slut. Hasn't she?" She pumps her two fingers in me, and I moan for release.

"Mistress, please. More. I'm right there. I don't know how I got so wet. Mistress, please touch my clit. Make me cum?" I hear the begging whine in my voice, and then I'm crying. I have no idea why.

"No, no. Not yet," she says casually, ignoring my sudden tears. "Not until later this evening when the other Mistresses are here." She continues to pump me a few more times and then abruptly stops. She curls her fingers inside me and pulls them out that way. It's too fucking much. Oh. My. God. Her fingers are out, and I'm breathing hard. "Pull your cheeks wider apart, whore." I do and then feel her wet fingers rubbing around my tiny hole. She pushes a finger in, and my breath catches in my throat. Oh, fuck. That feels so good. She pushes her finger in as far as possible and then pulls it out slowly, only to push back in again. I close my eyes and let my head drop and give in to her rhythm.

"Miss," I say and know the word isn't right. "Misstruh," I try again, but it's no better.

"Yes, whore?"

"Feels so good, Mistress," I manage to get out in between pants.

She pulls out her finger, and I'm momentarily disappointed until she introduces two fingers into my virgin ass. She is opening me up, but I can't take much more. "Mistress, let me cum, please." I moan as an involuntary pulse spikes through my cunt. She ignores me and pumps a few more times. Just as suddenly, she pulls both fingers out, and I feel abandoned. Empty.

She reaches to the table again and then rubs something cold around and in my tiny hole. "Whore," she addresses me, "I'm inserting a small butt plug. It will feel huge to you, but I assure you it is not, and your ass will adjust to it." I feel the tip of something at my hole. "I've used plenty of lube. Ready?"

I have no choice but to be ready. I say nothing. She smacks my already sore ass making me cry out. "Yes, Mistress. I'm ready."

"Ready for what, slave?"

"I'm ready for you to impale me on whatever the fuck a butt plug is." I exhale loudly and then add, "Mistress."

I feel the tip again, and then she pushes it inside me slowly. My tight ring of muscle protests the intrusion, and it starts to hurt as she pushes. "Yellow," I say, and she stops. Good to know she honors safe words.

"We'll pause for a moment and let your body adjust, but you'll be all right, pet. I promise." After what seems like no time, she pushes in a little bit more and pauses again before I can call yellow. Whatever she's pushing into me seems to get bigger as it goes. It's stretching and filling me. I feel violated. I breathe through the pain as she pushes in and pauses several times more until she finally announces that it's entirely in. I feel something like a base against my hole. Maybe this is to make sure the object doesn't get lost up there forever. My ass pulses around the plug, and as I catch my breath, I realize it's starting to feel okay. No, it feels more than okay. It kind of feels good.

"Color, pet?"

"Green," I say. "I think."

She laughs. "You did well."

"How long do I have to –"

"A few hours."

"Hours, Mistress?"

"Yes. We'll put the bigger ones in after lunch."

"Bigger *ones*?" I blurt. "Plural? Mistress? Really?" I groan. There's no fucking way.

She just laughs and says, "Get up and don't lose that plug." I'm so shaky that she has to help me up. I finally find solid ground and take a few breaths to steady myself. I feel like I have a pole stuck up my ass. It's such an odd sensation. She pulls up my new boi shorts, and if I lose the plug now, at least the boi shorts will hide that fact. "Phew, all that work has given me a huge appetite," she says. "Best get working on my cheese omelet, pet." She heads to the sink to wash her hands.

I spot two more butt plugs on the table. They are huge. *That's* what is going inside me later? I try to swallow, but I have no saliva. "Um, Mistress, may I please get some water first?"

"Yes."

I carefully go down to my knees in front of my water bowl and take a sip. My butt is raised up and on display, and I'm sure my Mistress is taking in the full view. I'm amazed the plug isn't pushing itself out. But then again, I'm *not* surprised. This fucker almost feels like it's expanding inside of me. I wiggle my ass, trying to make it fit more comfortably. It doesn't. I drink slowly. I *do* need the water, but I also need a minute to regroup. Mainly because I'm now horny as hell and not allowed to do anything about it. This must be my punishment because my Mistress is torturing me—all before breakfast.

I stand up and join her at the sink to wash my own hands.

She reaches behind me and rubs my very sore ass over my boi shorts. "That was nice, Bernadette. Got me a little wet, too." She leans close to my ear and whispers, "I might just make use of that tongue of yours later this afternoon. Upstairs. Before the Mistresses arrive."

"Really?" I can't keep from grinning.

"Would you like that, my little whore?"

I nod and then flashback to her hands, wrapping around my throat. "Yes, Mistress." I drop to my knees in front of her and place my face inches from her sex, hidden behind silk pajama bottoms. "I can start now, Mistress."

"Such an eager little pet. You're learning what it means to be a good slave, aren't you? That satisfying your Mistress's needs are your only goals." She latches on to my earlobe and pulls me up. "Later, pet. Right now, you need to feed us. You, especially, are going to need energy today. The other Mistresses will want *all* of you. And more."

Chapter Twelve

Pushing Boundaries

Not only am I exhausted from having slept in a dog bed on the floor, but the spanking on Mistress Ciara's lap also took a lot out of me. Thankfully she let me eat breakfast at the table with her. I thought for sure she was going to make me eat from a plate on the floor. And I would have. That thought alone disturbs me and makes me wonder how brainwashed I am already. I must be careful not to lose myself while I'm here.

During breakfast, Mistress Ciara tells me about service submission and outlines my chores for the day. So, apparently, in addition to being a slut and a whore, I am now a service submissive. First, I clean her master bedroom and bathroom thoroughly as instructed, and then she directs me downstairs to clean the guest bathroom. The kitchen is next. I am allowed brief rests, thank goodness, mostly in front of my water bowl on my hands and knees.

"Come into my office, pet," Mistress Ciara calls to me softly from down the hall. I stand up from my water dish and bring my bucket of cleaning supplies with me. Her office is a spare bedroom which has an office set up on one side. There is an extensive calendar spread out on a floor-to-ceiling bulletin board. Tacked to the board are pictures of people. There are a couple dozen men and a half-dozen women. They are all smiling. The calendar also has times listed on it. I take a glance at November and see my name. It says, "Dinner. crystal. Black Oak." I look back a few days and see my name listed at 7:00. My name is sandwiched in between other people's names. So now I know. I *was* an appointment. My time with her was just one of many.

"Do you make money at this?" And when all those words are out of my mouth, I realize what I've done.

Mistress Ciara whips her head around, and she stands up. She marches right up to me, her face inches from mine, and then reaches behind me and smacks my ass three times. I stand there and take it.

The pain is not pleasant this time. It is a definite reprimand.

"Go get the middle-sized plug and the lube from the kitchen table, slave."

"Yes, Ma'am." I leave quickly to do as she has bidden. Why am I such an idiot? Why didn't I keep my mouth shut? But then I realize something. She never answered my question.

I snag the middle-sized plug off the table and grab the lube. I've never seen lube before and note the brand and size for later reference.

"Pull your panties down to your ankles." I do so and stand back up. She walks up behind me and presses her body against my back. She reaches around and glides a hand down my stomach and over my smoothly shaved mons. A finger slips over my clit and then through my slick folds. She pulls the wetness back up and over my growing clit. I involuntary spread my legs and press my pelvis into her hand. She pulls back and smacks my mons, thankfully missing my clit. "Bend over and grab your ankles." I spread my feet apart and bend my knees just enough to keep my balance. With a twist of her wrist, she slowly extricates the smallest plug from my ass. It is pure heaven as it moves. Within moments she coats my tiny hole with cold lube and then presses the medium-sized plug at my entrance. With steady pressure, she pushes in. This time my body is ready to receive it, and I do so without calling a safe word. It fills me up, but it is not that uncomfortable. Once it's in, she gives it a final twist and then smacks my ass cheeks three more times.

"I should make you wear a ball gag," she says. There is anger in her voice. "But I won't. Clean this room." She leaves, and now I am alone.

I pull my boi shorts back up and get back to work. I don't dare look at her bulletin board again or any of her private information. I dutifully dust her overflowing bookshelves and the furniture. I have to move some papers on her desk, but I am sure to put them back exactly where they were.

The last thing I do is vacuum. I take one final look and am proud of my handy work. I've never done housework in just a bra and boi shorts before, and definitely not with a huge butt plug inside me, but there's always a first time. I know the living room will be next, so I wheel the vacuum and carry my supplies to that room.

"Make me lunch," Mistress Ciara says from her recliner in the living room. "I've put out a can of soup and sandwich makings. Make yourself food as well. I will eat in here. Slaves eat in the kitchen."

"Yes, Ma'am." I know she can hear the dejection in my voice. I am truly heartbroken. What an idiot I am for asking that stupid question. I won't be surprised if she makes me leave.

After making and then serving her lunch in the living room, I eat some soup and half a sandwich at the lovely table in the kitchen. I know I should eat more, but my stomach is in knots. After lunch, I clean up and then head to the living room to work on the last room. As if avoiding me, she has retreated to her office.

As I'm dusting the living room, I notice several weird metal hooks attached to the wall and various pieces of furniture, but I don't dare ask what they are for. I simply dust and then vacuum around them. Eyebolts! That's what they're called. As I clean, I notice that my car keys are still lying on the shelf where she placed them before I stripped off my clothes at her command last night. It was good to know that I could, indeed, leave at any time.

I have never given my new apartment this thorough a cleaning, and I can't remember when I'd ever given my house as thorough a cleaning either. And God knows what Jen is doing to my house now. I really must go over there and get November's rent check. November is almost over.

131

She is a real ass for not getting me my money. It's my house, after all. *Then why aren't you living in it?* a voice inside me asks. I suddenly feel dizzy and grab on to the big-screen TV.

"Put those things away. You're done." I jump at her voice and then do as I'm told. To finish up, I wash my hands in the kitchen sink. Without a word, Mistress Ciara attaches a leash to my leather collar, the one she put on me after my spanking. She pulls on the leash, making my head jerk forward. I have no choice but to follow. "We're going to play for a little while, and then you can rest before your big night with the Mistresses."

Once in her bedroom, my boi short panties and bra are yanked off, and within seconds she is removing the medium butt plug and inserting the biggest. I almost call yellow, but my muscles relax around the intrusion. Once the plug is inserted, she washes her hands and then takes off her pajama bottoms. She lays on the bed and then pulls me by the leash to join her. Within seconds, my face is buried in her pussy.

"Mistress?" I ask, stopping mid-task. I have to find a way to get her in a better mood. Besides making her cum, that is.

"Mmm," my Mistress murmurs. "Yes, whore?"

"You said the other Mistresses are going to use me. Does that mean, um, more than one at a time, Mistress?"

She peers down her body at me. "Most definitely, yes."

"Mistress?"

She sighs. "Yes, pet?"

I melt. She called me 'pet.' Maybe she's not mad at me anymore. "Will they use my tiny hole, too, Mistress? I've never..."

"Oh, they'll want to. But that's mine, all mine. Tiny holes are BBC's favorite. That's why the biggest butt plug is shoved up your ass right now. To stretch you. The other Mistresses are going to watch while I take your ass virginity." She reaches for my head.

Before she can shove my face back into the folds of her very wet pussy, I blurt, "I'm sorry for what I said before, Mistress. I wasn't thinking. I am an idiot."

"You are a submissive who forgot her place for a moment, that is all."

Am I out of the doghouse? I can't tell. "Mistress, you'll make sure the others aren't rough, right? They know my safe words?"

"Yes. Mistress Nikki is a bit of a sadist, but I'll make sure she leaves no permanent markings or blood."

"Blood, Mistress?"

"Don't worry, pet." She reaches down and tousles my hair, making me melt some more. "Why, oh, why has my silent Bernadette finally found her voice at this most inopportune time?" She smiles down at me and then shoves my face back to her pussy. "Lick me, slave."

I lick and suck and nibble for all I am worth. I think I have been forgiven. It doesn't take long before my Mistress has my head clamped between her strong thighs as she cums. I can do nothing else but go along for the ride. After forever, she finally releases my head. I roll it around, hoping I haven't sprained anything.

"We're both going to nap now, pet."

"Mistress, can I sleep on the bed with you?"

"Of course. Right where you are between Mistress's legs where every slave should be."

~~~

I wake up when a hand clamps over my mouth and my face is pushed into the bed. I try to pull away, but I can't as my legs are shoved apart. Something plunges into my cunt, and I grunt. The hand over my mouth grips more tightly. "Just a taste of this evening, pet," my Mistress whispers in my ear. Holy fuck! I wasn't expecting this. I was sleeping. How can I give consent if I'm sleeping? I struggle and pull away from her, but this only makes her laugh. She takes her hand away from my mouth. I know I can call my safe word, but I don't. For some reason unknown to me, this is thrilling.

Strong arms push me into the bed to keep me still. The butt plug in my ass alongside the BBC in my cunt is almost too much. I shift my body in an attempt to make it more comfortable, but then she throws her entire body weight on me as if to possess me. She is a big woman at five foot ten. She slides the dildo in and out of my body. She whispers in my ear, "So fucking wet, you whore. You dreamt about your Mistress in your sleep, didn't you?"

I'm breathing so hard from the adrenaline that it takes a minute to catch my breath. When I do, I am finally able to find her rhythm. She pulls me up onto my knees and grabs my hips firmly. A few sharp slaps sting my already sore ass, sore from the spanking I got in the kitchen before breakfast. "It's good to know there's a little fight in you, Bernadette. The Mistresses will love that." She continues to slam into me, my hips absorbing the force. My heart is still pounding as I relax into her rhythm. Getting fucked while sleeping wasn't one of my hard limits. Stupid naïve me didn't realize it was even something my Mistress would consider doing. And as I'm taking it, something incredible starts happening. I can't help it; I lean forward and lift my ass high in the air like a cat in heat so that she can pound me more deeply.

My Mistress laughs in victory. "The truth comes out. My whore likes CNC, doesn't she? Consent Non-Consent."

Her words tickle my mind. I don't ever remember giving consent to this. It doesn't matter at the moment, and I move my hips to match her rhythm. And now naïve me knows what the acronym CNC stands for. Consent non-consent. Rape fantasy. I can't think about whether or not I like it because, amazingly, I'm close to cumming.

"Almost there, whore?" she whispers in my ear.

I moan my response. She knows my body well at this point, and in one swift move, pulls out. I cry out at the shock. She smacks one of my ass cheeks and says, "Be in the shower in one minute."

I'm panting. She had me so close to cumming. She is the goddamned mother-fucking queen of edging, and I have somehow been led to worship at her feet.

I feel my wetness on my inner thighs as I scooch off the end of the bed and head to the shower. It isn't long before she joins me and turns on the water. It's cold at first, but then it warms up nicely. I'm a little cold, but I'm close to her. I'm only feeling the spray after it hits her body, but that's okay. Will she ask me to bathe her? *That* kind of service I can fully get into. Her full breasts are right there for the taking, but I can't touch her unless she permits me. *C'mon, Mistress*, I plead silently, *let me run my hands over your dark skin.*

Instead, she says, "Sit." I sit. I know the shower floor is clean because I scoured it spotless just a few hours ago. She luxuriates under the warm spray while I sit on the cold tile, shivering. She points to my pelvis. "Where did you get those bruises?"

"The kitchen table. Last night."

"Oh," is all she says. She steps forward and places her feet on the outside of my thighs, effectively pinning me. She moves so her pussy is inches from my head. "Open your mouth wide, slave." She positions her pussy over my mouth. "Make a tight seal around me and suck." When she moans, I know I'm doing something right. She puts both hands behind my head, pressing me to her. "Keep the seal," she commands after a minute. "I'm relaxing my body now." She moves her pussy around my lips slowly. "It would be so easy, Bernadette. So, so many slaves have sat right where you are, and they eagerly drink my nectar. But not you. Apparently, you're too good to drink your Mistress's nectar, but wear it, you shall." She moves her sex off my face, and before I realize what's happening, she releases her bladder, and a stream of hot yellow piss lands on my breasts and trickles down my torso. It pools on the tile between my legs where I sit.

"Mistress!" I try to scramble to my feet, but a quick slap to my right breast steals my flight response. "Mistress," I whimper weakly as the last of her urine trickles off my breasts. "This was a hard limit."

Danielle Grainger

"You wanted your boundaries pushed, slave. You told me that explicitly. At dinner on Wednesday. The dinner I paid for."

"But Mistress." I groan and then close my eyes as tears flow. This is so unfair. She's pushing all my limits, even the ones I didn't know I had. If the Mistress I trust – thought I trusted – does this kind of thing to me, then what are the other Mistresses going to do? Maybe I should call my safe word, get dressed, and drive home. What the fuck am I doing here, anyway? Why did I think I wanted this?

While I'm having a mental breakdown crying on the shower floor of a woman I met less than four days ago is humming and soaping up her body. This black woman, the one I call Mistress, CNC'd me and then marked me with her bodily fluids. And now she's humming.

The water goes off, and she opens the shower door and steps over me to get out. I hear her humming in the bathroom and then humming in her bedroom. I still can't move. The stink of her urine all over my body has me positively paralyzed.

I hear her come back into the bathroom. "You have a very generous twenty minutes to get ready for the Mistresses' arrival, whore. Do your enema first." Great, an enema. Because my day was going so well up until this moment. "The box is on the counter." She points, and my eyes follow. "Be thorough." Her dark eyes narrow as she says, "Very thorough. Shower after that. I'll put your collar, cuffs, and chains on you downstairs. These are the only things you will be wearing."

Chains? That's great, just great—the highlight of my day. I want to get up as she commands, but my muscles won't move.

She rushes into the shower and, with one hand, grabs me by the throat. "Do you understand me, slave?" Her dark, laser beam eyes skewer me.

"Yes, Mistress, I understand," I mutter.

She lets go of my throat with a push, and the back of my head clunks against the tile. It is only when my Mistress turns that I see what she holds in her other hand. Not one, but three black dildos of different sizes. Fuck. BBC has sisters, and the Mistresses will be here in less than an hour.

Chapter Thirteen

Nik

Mistress Ciara's eyes never leave me as I step into the kitchen after my lovely enema and my shower. Three BBC dildos lay drying on the table in front of her. Since my arrival last night, she's been talking about my three holes and how she intends to fill each one simultaneously. And in half an hour, two more Mistresses will be arriving. That will make three. My body already hurts from the thought.

Four leather cuffs sit on the table. Two will soon be around my wrists, that I know. I'm sure the other two are for my ankles. Oh, God, am I going to be chained up somewhere? Unable to defend myself? At the mercy of three Mistresses with dildos? Adrenaline spikes through me, and I visibly shudder. My Mistress smiles but doesn't comment. Next to the cuffs is a collar. It's different than my other two because this one is sturdy brown leather with four D-rings evenly spaced around it. Oh, great, now she can attach my leash from any side. But what's even more disturbing are the shiny metal chains laid out in rows on the table. One-, two-, three-, and four-foot lengths of metal.

This is too much. I swallow hard and look at my water bowl on the floor.

"Go ahead. Get some water, whore," she says to me coldly. She's getting into game mode, I think. She wasn't this cold when I arrived last night or even this afternoon when I said that stupid thing in her office. She started getting frosty right after that.

I get down on my hands and knees and lean over to lap at the water in my bowl. Let's face it; this is a dog dish. It's nothing more than that, and it's meant to demean me and remind me that she holds all the power. I am her white slave. I am her whore. I can't look at her right now. After what she did to me upstairs, I just can't. Not yet. I'm not sure I trust her anymore. I could simply say my safe word right now, stand up, put my clothes on, and head out the door. But I don't. I can't. I hate to admit this, but I need more of whatever she's offering.

Her chair scrapes on the kitchen tile as she stands up. Within seconds I feel her behind me as I kneel on all fours in front of my bowl. I don't turn around to look. A cold hand covers one of my ass cheeks and then kneads the flesh. "Soon, my BBC will be lodged in this white ass." Both of her hands move lower and stroke my inner thighs. My breathing gets heavy, and my body moves to her rhythm. This is the reason I'm not leaving. And she knows it.

She leans over me and whispers in my ear, "Horny little slut, aren't you?"

Her words alone make me moan, but I have no words for her. I don't need them. My body is doing all the talking.

"Sit up." I groan and do as she asks. She has been edging me all day, and it's as frustrating as hell. "Turn around and sit on that sore ass of yours." I do as I'm told and sit on the cold kitchen tiles. Bernadette Garneau *always* does as she's told. "Do you know why I'm putting these cuffs on you?" I shake my head. "It's for attaching chains to a white slave who doesn't know her place." She puts all four cuffs on me and has me stand up. She wraps one of the chains snugly around my waist and clips it tight with a double-ended snap hook, the kind you clip to a dog's collar. The next four chains are attached from my neck collar to my new chain belt. The metal is heavy. A set of shorter chains fastens my wrist cuffs to the belt. I can only move my arms about a foot away from my body.

"You look good, slave. Let me just…" She sounds like a sculptor examining the clay before her. No, wait, it's me we're talking about here. She examines the fine white *marble* standing before her. I must try to have a modicum of dignity somehow – if only in my head. "Yes," she says as if she's figured something out. She reaches for two more chains. One goes around my torso below my breasts, the other above capturing my breasts in between. She attaches them to the vertical chains running down from my collar. And, yes, this shit is freaking heavy. Bone-weary heavy.

I jump when she smacks my ass. She sits down on the kitchen chair and pats her lap. "Sit on my lap facing me, slave. Straddle my legs."

I do as I'm told. Her gaze penetrates me, and I can't look away.

"Mmm," she says. "You *are* a lot heavier. I like it, but I bet you don't. Slaves who are impertinent and don't know their place get chains. Isn't that right, pet?"

I want to look away, but when she raises her left eyebrow, I am mesmerized by the power of it. "Yes, Mistress," I finally say.

"You get chains today mainly because you dared to get nosy and ask questions about something you know nothing about. Many people, mostly men, pay top dollar for my services. It brings them relief. I'm not doing anything illegal. But I don't need to explain myself to you. Ever. Do you understand me?"

"Yes, Mistress," I say and swallow hard. "Again, I'm sorry."

"You are also in chains because you came when I told you to hold back your orgasm last night. Your little white cunt started spasming all over the place, saying, 'Fuck you, Mistress. I'll cum when I please.'" She pulls on one of the vertical chains causing me to fall forward into her. My head rests on her chest, and she wraps her arms tightly around me. Her mouth is right next to my ear when she whispers low, "And, tonight, you'll only cum when I tell you to. Tonight, your fucking white twat will *not* embarrass me in front of the other Mistresses. Is that understood?"

I swear she growls at the end of her words, so I blurt, "Yes, Mistress, I understand."

"Good." Her hands move from my back to my ass cheeks and squeeze my flesh. Hard. "Before I tell you what the other Mistresses will demand from you, let me reassure you, dear pet, that I am a professional Domme and that you will always be safe in my care." She exhales slowly into a sigh.

"Others pay for my services, but that's not our arrangement. Nor will it ever be." She pauses for a moment and adds, "Do you understand that I will make sure you're safe? Always?"

"Yes, Mistress. Thank you." I have to believe her. There is no way I can go forward with the evening if I don't. "I believe you, Mistress," I say more for my benefit than hers.

"Good." She lets go of her tight grip on my bruised ass cheeks and caresses my back. She whispers all the things that Nikki might do to me and how I am to respond. She also says I need to role play and be attentive. If I do that, Nikki's sadistic side might not manifest. I blow out a sigh hoping Nikki isn't some fisting bondage Domme who wants to tie me up and whip me. I don't think I would be up for a whipping, but then again, whipping isn't one of my hard stops. Neither is fisting. Maybe I should make them hard stops. I can't work up the courage to say so.

My Mistress laughs and says, "Now Tatiana, on the other hand, will be Tatiana. She will lead you wherever it is she wants to take you. All I can tell you is to trust her and go with it. She will *not* hurt you." My Mistress laughs again. "Quite the opposite. She might kill you with kindness."

I have no idea what she means by that. Sensory play? Mommy/little play? Pet play? These are all things that I've read about but am not well versed in. And not knowing what's going to happen makes my pulse quicken. "You'll always be there, Mistress?"

"Yes, keeping you safe." She must have heard my nervous breath because she says softly in my ear, "Bernadette, you'll be all right. I promise." She laughs and says, "Well, you'll be all right until BBC smashes your tiny hole to bits." She slaps my ass again and says, "Get up and kneel by your water bowl, your back to the wall."

I do as she commands, and she clips my ankle cuffs to two eyebolts screwed into the baseboard molding. She has freakin' eyebolts everywhere.

"Eyes down at all times unless told otherwise." I lower my head and nod that I have heard her. My ability to speak has completely disappeared again. "And do not speak unless prompted by one of the other Mistresses or me. You, slave, are a vessel. A vessel for *our* use." I nod again and look down at my bare thighs.

The doorbell rings, and I whimper like a dog as a jolt of fear shoots through me. My Mistress chuckles evilly.

I hear my Mistress greet her friends in the other room and offer them bottled waters. At one point in our talks online, she told me that drinking, drugging, and Domination never mix. It is at this very moment that I understand why. Impaired thinking makes for injured submissives. Or worse.

I hear them head toward the kitchen. Toward *me*. My heart is pounding.

"Whatcha got here, Ciara?" one of the voices says.

"A little white slave I picked up," my Mistress says. "She's become addicted to black pussy. She worships it."

"Is that so?" the same voice says. The voice squats in front of me and reaches out to cup my chin. A quick jerk up, and I'm looking into a pair of hard dark brown eyes that look at me like I'm a piece of livestock to be inspected. "You got yourself a blonde-haired blue-eyed whitey, Ciara. Nice work." She pulls my head back down and stands up. This must be Nikki.

"Aww," a softer voice says. "Look up, precious. Come on, don't be frightened." I hesitate because no one in this house has ever called me *precious*. "It's okay, darlin'. C'mon. Look up." I look up into the softest, kindest, roundest face I've ever seen. This has to be Tatiana. Her light brown eyes are sympathetic as she looks into mine. She tousles my hair and says, "She's so cute, Ciara." I look up at my Mistress to see her reaction, and she raises that darn eyebrow at me again. What am I forgetting? Oh, yeah. I shoot my eyes down and focus on the chains connecting my wrists to my waist.

"Nik, do you want to take her for a ride first?" Mistress Ciara hands her my leash.

"Fuck, yeah." Nikki reaches behind and unclips me from the eyebolts on the wall. She attaches the leash to my collar and pulls me up to my feet.

She holds a harness and one of the dildos that was on the table. "C'mon, slut. I'm gonna take you for a ride on my dick. Would you like that?" She leads me into the living room.

"Yes," I say, not quite knowing how to address her.

She whirls around and looks me dead in the eye, which is hard for her since she's about four inches shorter than I am. I slouch a little to let her have the power. "Yes, *Nik*," she corrects.

"Yes, Nik," I repeat. Nikki is definitely a woman, but Mistress Ciara told me to refer to Nikki as *he*. Calling him *Nik* will make that easier. "I'm sorry, Sir. It won't happen again."

"Good. Make sure it doesn't." He leads me to the center of the living room to the exact spot where I licked Mistress Ciara to orgasm twice twenty-four hours before. I'm surprised to see that a mat has been laid out over the carpet. Mistress must have put it down when I was in the shower. This will obviously be our play area. "On all fours, slut."

I do as my new temporary Master tells me. My Mistress comes over with four sections of chain, and together they work to attach my ankles cuffs to the eyebolts embedded in the tv hutch. Now I know what they're for. I try but can't quite close my legs. The chains won't let me. My wrist cuffs are detached from my waist belt and then reattached to two eyebolts screwed into the couch legs.

Nik stands behind me. I can hear him fussing with his clothes and the harness. I exhale. I'm about to be impaled in one hole or another. My Mistress pulls on each of the four chains making sure I am secure. Satisfied, she moves to her recliner chair to watch. I like that she is in my line of sight. Even though my eyes are down, I can see her high-heeled feet. Tatiana takes a seat on the couch right in front of me.

Rough hands touch my skin. "Fine piece of meat you found here, Ciara." Nik rubs his calloused hands over my lower back. He sucks air through his teeth and says, "Mm-hmm. I'm going to sink my dick into your white cunt and pound you until you beg me to stop." His hands move up my back to my shoulders. He moves in front of me and pulls up on my leash. I lift my head, challenging the chains weighing me down, and I look up at him. His BBC stares me in the face. The dildo sticks out through the unzipped zipper of his pants. He tips BBC toward my face, but six or so inches away. He pulls on my leash. "Crawl for it, bitch." I move forward on all fours until the chains holding my ankles pull tight, and I can't make any more progress. "I know you want it, slut. Lean forward. Pull my dick into your mouth."

I lean forward like he asks, straining against the chains that hold me back, and latch on to the head of the dildo. "Suck. Suck me like you mean it." I swirl my tongue around the head and then suck as bidden. He pumps into me. I keep my throat relaxed as his in-and-out motion goes deeper inside my mouth. He finally hits the back of my throat, but, by some miracle, I don't gag. The first time. After that, he is relentless, and I gag with every push forward. I can't catch my breath. A hard snapping sound comes from my Mistress's direction, and Nik pulls out of my mouth. I hang my head and drool a little as I catch my breath. It just feels good to be able to breathe.

One of Nik's hands strokes my face gently. I think he means it as an apology for being so rough. The small gesture warms my heart toward him—a little. I don't know what he has in mind next. One of his hands trails along my body as he moves behind me. The hand comes to rest on the small of my back as he settles in. I feel the tip of his dick at the entrance to my cunt, which has been in a perpetual state of wet since I got here a day ago.

"Oh, so ready for me," Nik says. "Nice and slick." He strokes my ass with one hand and feeds the tip of his dick into my body. He slowly pushes in until he bottoms out against my cervix, causing me to moan. "Oh, yes," he says. "This whore loves her some BBC." He pulls out and then slams into me again. "Tell me how much you love it, whore."

"Yes, Nik. I love BBCs." I moan as he bottoms out again. "I love *your* big black cock, Nik."

He develops a good rhythm, and soon his strong hands grip my hips tight. "Open your legs wider." He slaps my ass, and I slide my knees apart as far as I can get them. He slaps my ass again. He pinches the flesh of my cheeks, causing me to cry out. He pinches again, and my Mistress snaps her fingers loudly. He stops. My heart swells. My Mistress truly is watching out for me.

"You just open your legs for any boy walking by. Don't you, slut?"

"Yes, Nik. Any boy."

"You just let them pound your cunt from behind."

"Pound me, Sir. Do it." He picks up speed and moves his firm grip from my hips up to my waist as he continues to fuck me. He then reaches around my body and grabs my breasts through the chains. He has one in each hand and pulls me upright as his BBC ravages me. The truth is, the friction is intoxicating. He reaches up to my throat and then rakes his fingernails down my chest, breasts, and torso, pulling on the chains as he does so. It hurts, but incredibly, it adds to the sensation, and I feel my already labored breathing increase. I am practically panting for release. "Fuck me, Daddy. Fuck me." Oh, shit. *Daddy*? Where did that come from?

Nik moans behind me at the word. I must have hit a nerve. He growls as he says, "That's my whore; take it for Daddy." He pushes me back down, and I have no choice but to fall forward on my elbows. I feel him swirl his thumb around in my juices and push at my tiny hole. He eases his thumb in slowly, and I try not to clench. He twists his thumb around and rests his four fingers on my ass. He closes his grip and then, using that hand, pushes and pulls me back and forth on his cock. I have no choice but to move with him.

"Oh, my fucking God," I say. The sensations are starting to overwhelm me. "Oh, Daddy, fill me. Slam me." Nik's moans are becoming as desperate as mine. "Cum inside me, Daddy-Nik." I wasn't role-playing. I wanted Daddy-Nik to fuck me until I passed out. "Daddy, you're so big. I can't take it." The first wave of pre-orgasm hits me. "Daddy, I'm going to cum. Daddy, let me cum. Oh, God. Oh, God." Nik plunges deeply into me three more times and then moans as he hits his own release. I am panting almost to the point of hyperventilating. As he slowly pulls out of me, I collapse on the mat. I swear to God, one flick of my clit and I will supernova. I am on overload. My only two tasks at the moment are to breathe and *not* to cum. Once the threat of hyperventilating is over, I look up at my Mistress. She is smiling at me. No, she is beaming. She is pleased. So am I. By some miracle, my white cunt did *not* betray me this time. Of course, who knows what Mistress Tatiana has in store for me.

Nik moves near my head and leans down. He strokes my cheek gently with the back of his fingers and then leans forward to kiss my face. "Thank you," he whispers in my ear. I can't help but smile.

The Mistresses let me rest for a little while, but I am facedown on the mat with my sex still exposed because the chains won't let me close my legs. Before long, the cold air conditioning on my ample wetness makes me shiver. Tatiana kneels by me in an instant. "Are you cold, baby girl? Mommy Tatiana will take care of you."

Baby girl? Oh. My. God. Tatiana is a Mommy. Oh, please, yes. Please let it be that. I nod and try to speak, but my throat is dry, and no words come out.

"Does my little girl need some water?" I nod again. "C'mon," she says, "sit up. Let's sit on the floor together with our backs against the couch." I forget that I am chained and try to do as she asks. The metal chains rattle against each other, and I can't move. I groan in frustration. "What's this?" Tatiana asks in a stern voice. "What did you do to make Aunt Ciara put you in chains? Were you a bad little girl?" Her expression is stern.

Her gaze penetrates my soul, and I lower my eyes immediately; I'm ashamed that she has seen me in chains. Oh, God. How did this woman get in my head so fast?

"You know what Mommy does to little girls that have been bad, don't you?"

I shake my head. I don't think I want to know.

Chapter Fourteen

Mommy Tatiana

"Nik, unchain baby girl's ankles, won't you?" Mommy Tatiana says. Nik doesn't answer, but I feel his strong hands on my calves as he unclips the cuffs from the eyebolts embedded in the TV hutch. I automatically close my legs and pull them up under me. I haven't been able to do that since Mistress Ciara and Nik chained me down earlier. Having my private parts on public display and so very available was starting to freak me out a little.

Mommy Tatiana unclips one of my wrist cuffs but not the other. "C'mere, sugar." She tugs at my chain vest to pull me closer. I sit next to her on the floor, our backs against the couch. She hands me an opened bottle of water, and I thank her and then drink until I am satisfied. She takes the water bottle from me, and before I know it, I'm pulled into and then cradled in her fleshy but warm arms. Her embrace is somehow soothing.

"Now, little girl," she says to me quietly as if this is for my ears alone, "in a little while, you'll have to tell Mommy why Aunt Ciara put you in chains this weekend. You must have done something bad, something naughty." She exchanges a glance with my Mistress, but I cannot read what the exchange means. I'm not sure what to say to Tatiana, so I stay mute and lower my gaze. "Before we get into that bad stuff," she says, "come give me a proper greeting." She puts her hand under my chin gently and tips my head up. Her eyes are kind, so I lean closer and we kiss. The kiss is gentle and soft. "Mmm, baby girl's kisses are sweet," she murmurs and leans in for another.

This time her tongue ever so slightly dips into my mouth, and I welcome it. The entire time I have been here, Mistress Ciara has not kissed me, and I now realize how much I miss kissing someone. A warm brown-sugar wave of excitement runs through my body, and I hear myself moan as our kiss deepens. Her lips are soft yet quite insistent, and it isn't long before her tongue thrusts in and out of my mouth.

All at once, she pulls away and says in a flustered voice, "Ooh, baby girl, you are some kisser." She turns toward my Mistress and says, "Ciara, is it warm in here?" She looks back at me and fans herself. I smile at her theatrics. "Ahh," she says to me, "there's my little girl's smile. Look at that dimple." She pulls me close, and my head now rests on the shelf of her ample breasts. "You are a quiet one, aren't you? Now, c'mon, tell me why you're in chains."

And just like that, my shame is back. I groan in embarrassment, but this woman who claims to be my Mommy Domme makes clucking sounds of reassurance. I've done a lot of reading about Mommies and littles on *Kinks*, and apparently, it's not some kind of freaky incestuous pedophile fetish. No, instead, it's quite charming. The Mommy figure is the Dominant, just like Mistress Ciara is my Dominant. But Mommies and Daddies in the BDSM world also take on caregiver roles. Some of these Big/little relationships don't even have a sexual component to them at all. That perplexed me when I first read about them. I thought everyone on *Kinks* was there for sex. Little did I know that affection, attention, guidance, and simply the need to be seen and heard are paramount to most Big/little relationships. This is sometimes the only thing a person wants. Mistress Tatiana is very nurturing, but she is obviously also here for the sex. And so am I.

"Whisper it in my ear, little one. Tell me what you did wrong."

She seems so sincere that I don't hesitate, and I whisper to her how my white cunt decided to have an orgasm all on its own when Aunt Ciara was fucking me over the kitchen table. I told her that I didn't have permission to cum. I don't tell her about the stupid thing I said in Aunt Ciara's office, however.

"Oh, that was bad of you to defy Aunt Ciara that way." She pulls on my chains. "She was right to put you in these. You deserve her punishment, don't you?"

"Yes, Ma'am," I say and look down. I feel my face getting warm from embarrassment.

"I know what will make you feel better," she says to me, lifting my chin again. Her smile already makes me feel better. "Unbutton Mommy's blouse, dear. That's it. You've gotten so good at buttons." I beam at her praise, even if it is so oddly ludicrous to praise me for knowing how to undo buttons, but I go with the flow. I have to. She leans forward so that she can take off her blouse. She twists her back toward me and says, "Unhook my bra, baby." I do so, and her massive breasts spill out of her loosened undergarment. She pulls the bra off and throws it on the couch. Her leggings and panties quickly following. I somehow feel better that I am now not the only one who is entirely naked.

"Kiss me, baby," Mommy Tatiana commands, and I do. Her kisses are steamy, if not steamier than the first ones, and I find myself getting more aroused. As if that is even possible. She pulls back from our kiss and lifts one of her massive breasts toward my lips. I kiss her flesh and use my tongue to trace her large dark areola. Her breath catches when I suck her nipple into my mouth and run my stiff tongue over it. "Yes, yes, yes, baby girl. You know what Mommy likes. Don't you, little one?"

"Mm-hmm," I say around a mouth full of her flesh. I switch breasts when she offers the other one to me.

"Suck like you mean it, girl." She moans and then arches against me so that I am pulled tighter against her body. "Drink your fill, little one. Drink." I stay at her breast and suckle. I thank the Gods that she is not actually lactating. The thought of me drinking human breast milk gives me a bit of an ick factor, even though I know this is a fetish for many people. I run my stiff tongue over her nipple. Mommy Tatiana moans, and

I think she just might have an orgasm from this. After a while, she gently pushes my head away and breathes heavily for a few moments. Finally, she pulls me up for another steamy kiss.

After searing me with her lips, she says, "Time to do your homework, baby." I have no idea what *homework* she's referring to, but I go along with it. "Let's practice on Mommy's special spot." She lays herself down on the mat and pulls me on top of her. At first, I think she wants me to kiss her again, but then she pushes my head down. I can't linger on her breasts either because she pushes me lower still.

"Mmm, yes, little one. Go on. You know where Mommy's special spot is." I kiss the folds of her ample belly on my way down.

"Mmm," she moans. "Lower, baby. You know Mommy's special place. Go on now. Like I've been teaching you."

I kiss down her abdomen and decide to tease her a little. I may get in trouble for it, but how much more trouble can I get in? I'm already in chains and attached to the furniture. I lick her belly button and say, "Is this the special spot, Mommy? Right here?" I kiss it again.

The cutest unintelligible sound comes out of her mouth. "Have you forgotten your lessons already? Lower, baby. Lower."

I kiss further down and plant a kiss on one of her hip bones. "Here?" I ask but don't want to press her patience, so I move on and kiss the top of her fleshy mound. She, too, is shaved clean. "How about here, Mommy?"

Mommy Tatiana spread her legs a little. "Almost, baby girl. Lower. Lick Mommy like I taught you." My whole core weakens at her words. A shot of adrenaline rushes through me. Oh, my God, this is heady stuff. I settle in between her thighs, my chained arm holding on to her thighs.

I'm not sure if this will get me in trouble or not, but I decide to talk to her. "Mommy, you're so brown everywhere except in the center, right here. It's so pink and wonderful. May I lick you there, Mommy?" I put on what I hope is an innocent-looking expression and look up at her from where I lay between her legs. Her glistening wetness is inches from my lips. "May I lick your pink?"

"Oh, such a good baby girl." She moans and adds, "Yes, little one, you have permission to lick my pink."

I beam at her as if I have been offered candy before dinner and then dip my head toward my appointed task. Her puffy lips show her excitement, but instead of licking where she expects me to, I tease her by trailing my tongue down one inner thigh and back up the other. She squirms in anticipation, and I finally acquiesce and lick her outer lips. I taste her juices. This is a taste I had been denied in my life for quite some time now. It is finally dawning on me what a gift this weekend is. I pull her inner lips into my mouth and gently suck them causing her to moan passionately. She reaches down and runs her hands through my hair but doesn't force me to her clit. Not yet, anyway. I swirl my tongue around her opening and then plunge my tongue inside her. Her hips start undulating gently. She likes this. I spend a few more moments licking the inside of her folds, enjoying her flavor, and then I pull out. She is breathing heavy, and it won't be long before I make her cum.

My one hand remains shackled to the couch, but with my free hand, I reach under her leg and pull myself closer to her. One of her legs ends up on my shoulder, and this allows me to dig into my work. I hear a few quick snaps from my Mistress, and then my other wrist is unshackled. I quickly pull Mommy Tatiana's other leg over my shoulder and splay my hands on her stomach. Her earthy scent is almost sweet. She moans encouragement to her baby girl, and I lick my way all around her folds, intentionally missing her clit, which is fiery red and demanding attention. I've never seen a clit grow that big and fat before. It's time. I dive in and capture it between my lips and rub the tip with my tongue. I leave her clit momentarily and reach down with my tongue to pull more wetness up from her folds to her clit. I am in absolute heaven licking her pussy, and so is she.

Mommy Tatiana's hands fly to the back of my head, keeping me in place. "Stay right there, baby girl. Right there at Mommy's special place." I pick up my pace and swirl my tongue around her clit and then up and down. "Yes, baby girl," Mommy Tatiana's voice has gotten deep with need. She's almost there. Her hand reaches down and unwraps my arm from around her leg. She grabs two of my fingers and shoves them in her pussy. "Pump, baby. Pump Mommy's pussy. And keep licking like Mommy taught you."

I work my fingers in and out of her slickness. I curl them up and try to hit her g-spot with every outward pull. All this while continuing my tongue workout on her clit. It isn't long before she arches her back and crushes my head between her thighs. Even though her thighs encase my ears, I still hear her screams of passion. It is a beautiful sound, and I am so proud that I brought her to that place.

My ass has been up in the air and on display this entire time, and without warning, Nik pushes two fingers inside my cunt. He pumps me as I continue to lick Mommy Tatiana clean as instructed. Mommy Tatiana finally reaches down and pulls my head away. Apparently, she is finished. "That's my good girl," she coos at me. "You will be rewarded." She is breathing heavily as she tells me this.

I hear her words, but Nik's fingers are taking my attention. I move my body backward to meet his movements. I want him deeper inside me. "Mommy," I say to Mommy Tatiana, "I'm so ready to cum. Is it okay? I've been good. Nik is –" I moan as he increases his pace.

"Nik's fucking you with his fingers. Isn't he, sweetie?" Mommy Tatiana asks. "He must know what a good girl you've been and wants to reward you. But this is Aunt Ciara's house, and she has something exceptional planned for you. Right, Nik?" It's clear by the tone in her voice that she wants him to stop.

"Yeah," he says and stops pumping me. He pulls his fingers out of my cunt and swirls my juices around my small hole. "Ciara is going to take your last virgin hole. Ain't that right, Ciara?"

Just as Nik asks the question, he pushes one finger in my small hole and pumps that. I am melting at his touch and lay my head down on Mommy Tatiana's mound. I'm sure she feels my warm exhales on her swollen sex. He pulls out and pushes in a second finger. I moan my pleasure. Two fingers turn into three, and there is nothing else in my world but his fingers pumping me in the ass.

"Oh, yes," Mistress Ciara says and sucks air between her teeth. She obviously likes what she sees. "There is a big reward for my pet." After a moment, she says, "Pet?"

It takes a moment for me to understand that she is talking to me. "Yes, Mistress?" I blow out my breath, trying to focus on her words. Nik continues to pump my ass.

"You've done well." She holds up three objects, and I almost choke. "These will be your reward." She holds the three BBCs in her hands.

I groan. It is time for them to wreck me completely.

Chapter Fifteen

You're Going to be Occupied

"Get up," Mistress Ciara says to me in a stern voice. I am not chained down anymore, so I can stand up freely. I keep my eyes down as instructed and wait. I'm not sure what to do with my hands, so I let my arms fall by my sides.

"Kitchen. Now." Mistress Ciara walks away from me.

"Yes, Mistress," I say and follow her. Even her walk is powerful, and she is in heels. I don't know how she pulls that off. I've never been able to wear heels in my life.

"Get water." She points to my dish on the floor. I get down on all fours, my chains clinking together as I do so.

"Come here," she says after I've had a few sips. "Drape yourself over my lap."

"Mistress, did I do something wrong?" I make no move closer. Am I about to get another spanking?

She raises her eyebrow at me. I hear Mommy Tatiana and Nik talking low in the other room. Thank God they are not here to witness whatever Mistress Ciara is about to do to me.

"On my lap, slave. I won't ask you again."

"Yes, Ma'am," I say and comply. I brace myself, unsure what I've done to deserve a spanking this time.

"I need to stretch you again," she says evenly. "Pull your ass cheeks apart."

I don't answer but do as I'm told. I feel the cold lube against my tiny hole and clench.

"Relax, pet," she says in a softer tone. "You'll be fine."

I urge my muscles to unclench, and then, after a moment, the largest butt plug is lodged in my ass again. This time I almost enjoy the insertion. This time the nerve endings down there send beautiful signals to my clit. There has been so much sensory input this evening that if she permits me to cum, I know I will either explode or pass out. Maybe both.

Mistress Ciara pulls me up and asks me to sit on her lap facing her. I do and feel her exquisite body warmth on my naked skin. One by one, she removes my chains. Ahh, relief. I feel so much lighter. However, she does not remove my wrist and ankle cuffs, nor does she remove my collar. "Look at me, pet."

I look into her gorgeous brown eyes, inches from my blue ones. Her gaze seems one part soft and one part hard. I want to kiss her so bad. My lips are so close to hers. She says, "You've done very well, pet. The other mistresses are pleased. I can tell." I feel my cheeks warm at her praise. "This next scene will be intense. Feel free to use your safe words. Call your colors at any time. Do you understand?"

"Yes, Mistress," I say. "I understand."

"There is no shame in it. I want to make sure my property remains safe. Always."

"Thank you, Mistress."

"And if your mouth happens to be full, then you are to snap your fingers. This will be the equivalent of red."

"Like you've been doing, Mistress?"

She smiles and says, "Yes, pet. Just like that." She reaches into the pocket of her skirt and hands me my cell phone. "Text your people. Let them know you're all right. You're going to be occupied for a while and won't have a chance later."

"Thank you," I say and hit the *Kinks* app to send Lisa a message that I am okay and having a fantastic time and that she'll get more details later. I even remember to include another of our agreed-upon secret words. While I'm doing this, my Mistress is kneading the cheeks of my ass. It is heavenly because it makes the butt plug move around, causing incredible sensations inside me. My breathing quickens as I finish my message to Lisa and then send another shorter one to Miss Olga.

"Finished?" Mistress Ciara says, and I nod. She takes the phone from me and then looks me in the eyes for the briefest of moments. Oh, my God, is she going to kiss me? "Nik, bring me the leash," she barks. I jump at the coldness of it.

When Nik enters the kitchen, Mistress Ciara commands, "Shackle this slave face down, plenty of slack."

"You got it," Nik says. He clips the leash to my collar and pulls me off Mistress Ciara's lap. My Mistress doesn't make eye contact with me even as I look her full in the face. Something just happened in her head, I'm sure of it, but I don't know what. My fight or flight adrenaline spikes, but I reassure myself that all will be well. So far, she has kept her promises about keeping me safe; I have to have faith in that.

Once again, I am chained to the mat, my ankles to the TV hutch, my wrists to the couch. I almost laugh out loud when I realize that her couch truly is lovely, indeed.

"I love that smile," Mommy Tatiana says and strokes my face. "Give us some sugar." She leans down for a kiss, and I close my eyes to kiss her deeply. I channel all of my nervous energy into this task. I feel better when she pulls back, less about to freak out. "Mmm," she says emphatically. "You are one seriously good kisser, little girl." I feel my face warm at her praise.

My Mistress walks into the living room. She is sporting a mischievous grin, probably because she is finally going to participate in this evening's wrecking-Bernadette festival. She looks at Nik and snaps her fingers. Whatever silent communication they have going on, I can't figure it out. All I know is that Nik is sporting the biggest of the three strap-ons and commands me to get up on all fours. This time there is plenty of slack in my chains. He shimmies himself underneath me and then tells me to sit up. My cunt is now positioned just over the strap-on he holds straight up toward my body.

"I'm going to fuck you good, blue eyes." He adjusts his cock so that the tip sits right at my entrance. "Let's go for a ride, cowgirl. Ease my cock inside you. Nice and slow."

"Yes, Sir," I say, and his eyes glow with lust at my words. I reach down and feed the tip into my slickness and then lower myself down on it. It is big, and with the butt plug still inside me, I am deliciously filled.

"Ride it, slave," my Mistress says from behind me. I can't see her. The only thing I see is her now-discarded high heels by the couch.

I have never ridden a cock like this, and it takes me a few tries to keep my balance and then get a good rhythm going.

"So good, Sir," I say to Nik as I lift myself up and down on his BBC. The girth of the dildo fills me as it rubs against the butt plug lodged in my ass. It is an incredible feeling. "You're so big, Sir. You fill me." He moans lustfully and then reaches up to massage and squeeze my breasts. He licks his lips as if he wants a taste, so I lean forward and fall on my outstretched hands, one hand on either side of his head. I angle my body so that my right breast hangs toward his mouth. He pulls my nipple into his mouth and sucks fiercely. I cry out at the lustful sensation and then yelp when he bites down hard. The pain goes straight to my clit, and I am losing sight of reality as I ride his cock and the pain simultaneously. A quick finger snap from my Mistress, and he releases my breast.

Nik grabs my waist and pulls my body down on top of him. Our bodies mold together. He holds me still and then grabs both ass cheeks as he takes over the thrusting. He can't get as deep at this angle, but it still feels fantastic.

"Look up at me, baby girl," Mommy Tatiana says. I squelch my groan as I see her sporting the medium-sized dildo. "Move over to the side a little so you can give Mommy a proper blow job." I move off to one side, both hands on the right side of Nik's body. Mommy Tatiana strokes my cheek

157

and then presses the tip of the dildo to my lips. "Take it like a good girl," she growls.

I am used to this sport by now and take it in my mouth. I like that this dildo is a little smaller than the one pounding my cunt. I keep my mouth slack, and Mommy Tatiana starts to move. She never hits the back of my throat, for which I send her a relieved thank you with my eyes. She receives my silent message and winks back at me, tousling my hair as she does so. She and Nik create a heady rhythm, and I am powerless to stop the orgasm that is building.

I have to somehow ask permission to cum, but my mouth is filled. Snapping. That's it. I reach out and snap the fingers of my right hand. All motion stops, and the dildo is pulled out of my mouth. I am breathless as I say, "I going to cum, Mistresses." It's building, and I moan as a pre-orgasmic wave runs through my body even though all movement has ceased.

"We're just getting started, pet," my Mistress says. "You'll have to find a way to hold on." Nik slowly pulls his BBC out of my body, and I try not to fall on him in relief. "Spread those cheeks for me, Nik," she says, and I feel Nik pull my flesh farther apart. I am still off to the side, so only one breast makes contact with him. I rest my head on my hands on the mat, getting ready for my impaling. "Head up, pet," Mistress Ciara says.

I lift my head and see that Mommy Tatiana is holding something in her hand. "Be a good girl and let Mommy put this blindfold on you." I don't resist, and she fastens it on nice and tight and then double-checks it. I cannot see a thing.

"What do you say to Tatiana, pet?" Mistress Ciara asks me.

"Thank you for blindfolding me, Mommy."

"Good girl," Mommy Tatiana says with a chuckle. And then she murmurs under her breath something I'm sure is meant only for me to hear, "You're a keeper, little one." In a normal voice, she says, "Aunt Ciara is going to take your virgin hole now, baby. Relax into it."

Mistress Ciara's hands touch my ass cheeks again. She rubs my skin and inhales through her teeth. "Mmm, BBC is going to love taking this white ass." She slowly pulls the butt plug out with a slight twist. The sensation is almost too much. Within seconds I feel the coldness of the lube. She rubs it into my hole. I try not to tense up. This will be the first time I will have a dildo in my ass, and she knows it.

The tip feels impossibly huge as it presses against my back door. She's using the smallest of the three dildoes, but it still feels mammoth. "Relax your body, pet. Don't fight me. We have all night."

Mommy Tatiana strokes my face soothingly and murmurs words of encouragement. I love this woman at this moment. I almost feel proud that she gets to witness this important milestone in my life.

Mistress Ciara kneels behind me, between Nik's outstretched legs. One of my Mistress's hands is on my hip. The other must be on the dildo, guiding it toward its goal. The pressure of the tip against my knot of muscle increases relentlessly. I am just about to call yellow when the head suddenly slides in. Mommy Tatiana cheers as if I've just scored my first goal in Pee Wee soccer.

Mistress Ciara then moves forward, and the dildo enters my body at a snail's pace. And that's okay with me. The butt plugs have stretched me, but this dildo-experience? It's way different. The silicone dildo slides over sensitive nerve-endings causing me to shudder.

"Color, pet?"

"Green, Mistress," I say breathlessly. "Green."

"Excellent." She continues the descent into my ass, and it isn't long before she's bottomed out. She must have signaled to the rest because a cheer goes up from Nik and Mommy Tatiana.

"Fuck her good, Ciara," Nik growls from underneath me. He still has a good hold on my ass cheeks.

My Mistress doesn't respond, but she pulls out a little and then pushes back in. I moan, low and deep. This is ecstasy. This is heaven. This is pure bliss. She slowly and rhythmically pumps my ass. I sigh to her rhythm. My body is heading toward a point of no return. My moans turn into pleas, "Mmmmmistress, please let me cum. My cunt is trembling –"

She ignores me entirely and says, "Fill that cunt, Nik."

In an instant, Nik's own BBC is at the entrance to my trembling center. He pushes into my body slowly as my Mistress continues the onslaught of my ass. They alternate thrusts so that when my Mistress pushes in, Nik pulls out and vice versa. It is the most incredible feeling in the world, and I moan with each thrust. My moans take on an urgent tone, and I find myself whimpering. By some miracle, I am not in the least embarrassed displaying my passion in front of these strangers.

The third BBC presses against my lips. I take the cock into my mouth, and I am on sensory overload. Every hole is filled. This was on my bucket list. Mistress knew that. But I can't focus on bucket lists because my body is building up to the biggest detonation in my life.

I moan around the cock in my mouth. I am on sensory overload.

"Color, pet?"

The cock leaves my mouth, and I swallow hard, trying to find saliva. "Green." I take this moment to catch my breath and then blurt, "I need to cum, Mistress." I barely get my sentence out when the cock fills my mouth, cutting off my pleas.

"Oh, you can hold on, pet," my Mistress says. "BBC just got into her favorite hole. Plunging inside of you is her favorite past time. In and out of your white ass. Opening all your holes to our big black cocks." Her words match her thrusts. I go along with the rhythm and somehow *do* hang on. But only for a moment.

A pre-orgasmic wave hits me, and my body shakes uncontrollably. A second pre-wave hits me. My cunt spasms, and yet I have not orgasmed. I'm going to blow any second.

Three sharp smacks hit my ass cheeks as my Mistress moans and then says, "Do it, pet. Do it. Cum for us. Cum all over our big black cocks. Show us how much you like getting fucked in every hole of your body."

Her words ignite me, and it only takes a few seconds before I am once again pulled into outer space and hung up in nothingness momentarily until hurtled back down to earth. I don't feel the cock leave my mouth, but it's gone, and I am shrieking in ecstasy as I've never shrieked before. My voice can be heard in heaven itself. My shrieks are *from* heaven itself. The remaining dildos in my body slow their pace.

That is the last thing I remember.

Chapter Sixteen

Scream for Me

Something soft is draped over me. A soothing voice whispers in my ear as an arm goes around me. "That was beautiful, baby girl." I feel Mommy Tatiana's body embrace mine.

"Mmmm," is all I can say. I am riding a blissful cloud of sensation. Her arms around me make me secure and floaty. This is the most beautiful high I have ever had. I moan my pleasure as another wave pulses through my cunt.

"Aftershock," my Mistress says from far away. Too far away if you ask me.

Mommy Tatiana strokes my face. "You are such a beautiful woman," she murmurs in my ear.

"Mmm," I say. She has broken character. I appreciate her humanity.

Another hand strokes my face. I can tell that it is Nik's hand by the roughness of it. "You did good, blue eyes," he says. "That was the best fucking orgasm I've ever heard." He chuckles, and Mommy Tatiana murmurs her agreement.

I feel hands remove my blindfold, but my eyes are glued shut, and I cannot open them for the life of me. A warm hand strokes my face again. It has to be Mommy Tatiana. I murmur, "Thank You, Mommy."

She makes cooing sounds and kisses my cheek. I could get used to this. I moan as another aftershock runs through me.

I hear a sharp finger snap and then hear Nik stand up. I soon hear them talking in low voices in the kitchen. I can't make out all the words, but I do hear Mistress Ciara say, "She's had enough, Nik. That's final. You still have a lot to learn about being a Dominant."

I smile as I hear that. My Mistress truly is taking care of me. Why did I ever doubt her?

"You have a beautiful smile," Mommy Tatiana says. "Tell me this, baby girl. Has Ciara kissed you?"

I shake my head.

"Tsk," she clucks. "That's too bad. I like you." She kisses my cheek once more, and then suddenly, her warmth and her comforting arms are gone. I hear her head toward the kitchen.

I snuggle into the blanket and sigh. I have still not opened my eyes. I doze off to the sounds of a quiet argument going on in the kitchen. It sounds like Mommy Tatiana is giving Mistress Ciara a stern scolding. I just can't stay awake long enough to find out why.

~~~

I wake to someone pulling on my earlobe. "Get up, pet," Mistress Ciara says. "You need to text your people."

I blink my eyes open and see that it is dark in the living room, where I still lay on the mat wrapped in a blanket. Someone even put a pillow under my head. Mommy Tatiana, probably.

"Mmm," I groan as I sit up. I sense that the other Mistresses are gone. I don't ask. "I'm sore, Mistress."

"I bet you are. You took quite a pounding." She chuckles and adds, "Be upstairs in three minutes."

"Yes, Ma'am," I say and yawn. She leaves me, and I hear her make her way up the stairs. I stretch my arms overhead, trying to wake up. I look at my phone and see that Lisa has messaged me. Shit, I am a half-hour past our agreed-upon check-in time. I send her a quick message back, including another one of our secret words, and tell her that I am in bliss. I tell her I will send her a message in the morning. I send Miss Olga a similar message, leaving out the bliss part.

I finally stagger to my feet and fold up the blanket I was wrapped in, only to discover that it is a Cleveland Browns blanket. If I'd known my Mistress was a Browns fan, this rival Bengals fan might not have made the trip up here. I laugh, knowing that is the farthest thing from the truth, but perhaps I will tease her about it later.

A jolt of adrenaline hits me when I hear her countdown begin upstairs. I pick my way up the stairs carefully in the darkness and realize that I am still wearing have my ankle and wrist cuffs. And my collar, too. Hopefully, she'll take them off me. I have welts where the leather has cut into my skin.

When I get to her bedroom, I hear the shower running in the master bathroom. I cringe remembering what she did to me in the shower earlier that morning. I stand near my pet bed, the only part of the room I can kind of claim as mine and announce that I am there.

She walks out of the bathroom, completely nude. "Come here, pet," she says softly. I do as bidden. She undoes my wrist and ankle cuffs and then takes off my collar. I rub my neck where I'm sure it has left marks.

"Go to the toilet if you need to, and then join me in the shower." She gestures in the direction of the running water. "I need to give you aftercare."

I read about aftercare on *Kinks* but never really understood it until now, standing in the shower with Mistress Ciara. She bathes me with a luxurious soft sponge over every square inch of my body. In her own way, she is making love to me, and I am positively swooning. She presses my front to hers, and I sigh into her arms. I moan my pleasure at feeling her skin against mine. It is heavenly. She washes my back and buttocks and then turns me around and asks me to bend over. She carefully cleans my private areas and is very gentle with my tiny hole. I can't help getting aroused and moan again.

"You are a sensitive pet, aren't you?" she says with a chuckle.

"Mm hmm," is all I can say.

She finally lets me go and washes her own body, and I am devastated by the emptiness. Finally, she rinses us both thoroughly and then shuts off the water. She steps out of the shower stall and hands me a towel. Once she finishes drying herself, she finishes drying me. I feel like a queen.

"How is my pet feeling now?"

"Blissfully loved, Mistress," I say.

She simply chuckles and says, "Tatiana would put me in time out if I didn't take good care of you." She hangs up both towels and says, "C'mon, let me get you to bed."

My heart soars as I naively think I will be able to sleep and snuggle with her in the big bed. But that is not to be. She leads me over to the dog bed and lifts the blanket for me to crawl under. I look up at her with what I know is a disappointed expression, but she seems unmoved.

"I have appointments tomorrow afternoon," she says matter-of-factly. "You'll have to be gone by eleven."

"Yes, Mistress," I say as evenly as I can, but her words are like a knife to the heart. "I understand." By some herculean strength that I did not know I had, I don't let my massive disappointment show. Instead, I manage to remain calm and even keeled like always.

"I have a few more things I want to teach you about being a proper submissive. That will happen tomorrow morning."

"Yes, Mistress," I say evenly. I try to keep my eyes open, but they are trying to close on their own. I am suddenly exhausted.

"And I am also going to fuck you silly tomorrow morning. BBC likes your white body too much to miss out on another round or two."

"Yes, Ma'am," I say. I hear the renewed enthusiasm in my voice, and I hope she hears it, too.

"Go to sleep. You need it."

"Yes, Mistress. Thank you for today. Good night."

There is no response.

~~~

"Get up," I hear. A shot of adrenaline hits me, and I struggle to unentangle myself from the blanket. I stand. It is morning, I can tell by the light streaming in from the bedroom window. "Why are your arms there?" She points to my arms crossed over my bare breasts.

"I'm cold, Mistress."

"Your needs don't matter, slave," she says sternly. A tight white shirt accentuates her dark cleavage, and a black skirt shows off her curves. "Put your arms straight down at your sides. Hands pressed to upper thighs." I do as she asks. "This, slave, is the *Attention* pose. Any time a Dominant asks you to stand, this is the pose you perform."

"Yes, Mistress," I say and look up at her.

"Eyes down," she barks at me. I flinch as my eyes shoot down. "If your Dominant wishes to inspect you, he or she might ask for an *Inspection* pose. Arms up, hands behind your head, elbows in the air, as if you are being arrested." I do as she asks. "Head up, but eyes down. Yes," she says with pride. "Legs apart, slave. This is part of your inspection." This time she walks around me, and for the first time, I see that she is carrying something in her hands. It is a riding crop. Oh, God, is she going to hit me with that thing? She walks behind me and says, "Spread your legs wider apart." The riding crop taps my inner thighs, and I spread my feet apart. My arms are still held overhead. I have to pee, but I don't dare tell her that. She is inspecting me, after all.

The crop slides up my right inner thigh until it's nestled in between the inner lips of my sex. She moves it front to back. "Will this come back wet as it is supposed to?"

"Yes, Mistress," I say. Just being near her makes me wet, but it is her Dominance that has gotten my juices flowing this morning.

She pulls the crop away and says, "Yes, you are slick. Good. All slaves' bodies must be ready and available to their Dominants at all times. Your body is available for my pleasure this morning, and I will do with it whatever I want. She walks up behind me. An arm reaches around my stomach, and she splays her fingers over my lower abdomen. She presses gently. I try to back up to relieve the pressure she puts on my bladder, but one sharp whack on my ass with the riding crop puts me right again. "Stand still, slave. I know you have to pee. You'll just have to hold it until I finish my inspection."

The pain is one part agony but is also one part pleasure. I squeeze the muscles inside me to ensure I do not have an accident on her bedroom carpet. She presses her body against my back and pulls me to her by my stomach, by my bladder. I moan in agony. I think she is taking perverse pleasure in torturing me. All at once, she releases me and says, "Go." She points to the master bathroom.

"Thank you, Mistress," I say on the run. I moan long and loud as I relieve myself. I can hear her chuckling in the bedroom at my expense.

"Mistress, may I brush my teeth and wash my face?" I figure I'd better ask before doing so.

"Two minutes."

Two minutes is plenty of time, and I am standing in front of her in the *Attention* pose well before she can even think of starting any sort of count down. In the short time that I was in the bathroom, I see that my Mistress shed her clothes and donned the biggest of the three strap-ons. She said I was going to get fucked this morning. Now is as good a time as any, I suppose.

"Nice, slave. Very nice," she says. "*Inspection* pose, please." I raise my arms, keep my head up but my eyes down, and spread my legs apart.

"Yes, good." I can't help but swell with pride at her praise. "Get on the bed. On your back. Head on the pillow, knees up, legs falling to the sides."

I do as I'm told and find that I am in a traditional missionary position open for impalement.

"Hands down at your sides on the bed, elbows bent. Yes, good. This is called the *Sex Doll* pose. Personally, I hate the name, but that's the accepted term." She climbs on the bed and forces my legs wider apart. "Are you ready to get fucked?"

"Yes, Mistress," I say.

"Good, because it wouldn't have mattered if you were ready or not. A slave's body is her Dominant's to do with what he or she pleases. And it pleases me to fuck you now."

She places the tip of her BBC at my entrance, and there is no slow insertion. She thrusts in quickly and pulls out just as fast. The mere friction has me pulling at the bedsheets as I try to hang on. She leans forward and puts her hands on my hips, her thumbs dig into my lower abdomen. My breasts bounce as she takes me hard. I reach up to grab them to hold them down.

She swats at one of my hands. "I want to see those white titties bounce." I place my hands by my side in the *Sex Doll* pose. In moments, an orgasm builds. Positioning me in submissive poses has aroused me incredibly.

My mistress continues to slide her BBC inside me. Her thumbs press into the bruises made from Friday's kitchen fucking, but the pain is somehow supplementing my pleasure. I still don't understand that. She shifts position and falls forward. Her hands land on my breasts. She squeezes my breasts as her rhythm continues. As she thrusts inside my body, my orgasm builds. I realize that throughout the weekend, she has been teaching me how to be a proper submissive. She has been grooming me. As I reach the point of no return, I think that maybe she wants to keep me. This heady thought enters my brain and sends a jolt right to my clit. I moan, and she pinches both nipples. Hard. It's too much.

"I'm going to cum," I moan. "I can't stop it."

"Cum for me, slave," she says as she continues to thrust and twist my sensitive nipples. "Let me hear your voice, Bernadette. Scream for me."

And I do scream as the wave hits me. I cry out until I am out of breath. Moan after moan escapes my lips as the aftershocks hit me. The aftershocks combined with the dildo pulling at the hood of my clit send me to new heights. Another smaller orgasm hits, and my body involuntarily goes fetal when my core clenches. I almost manage to knock my Mistress off of me, but not quite. It wasn't my intention, but my body had other ideas, apparently.

Mistress Ciara slows her pace and chuckles. "You're a good girl, pet." She pulls her BBC out, and I have a moment to catch my breath. But it's a very short-lived moment.

"*Table* pose, please," she says. I have no idea what she means, so I don't move. "Turn over and position yourself on your hands and knees." I do as I'm told and feel my wetness seep out of me and run down my leg. "Knees spread apart. Keep your sex available to your Dominant. Present your body to her. Put your arms further out in front, allowing both your vagina and ass to be accessible. Some Dominants want your head up, others down, and still others want your head in a perfect line with the rest of the body."

"Which would you like, Mistress?"

"Whatever is comfortable for you, pet." She spreads lube in and around my tiny hole. The tip of her biggest BBC is at the entrance. "We have not stretched you today. Breathe into it."

It is painful, I'm not going to lie, but my Mistress has proven over and over that she has my best interests at heart and won't hurt me. I've trusted her with my body, I've trusted her with my mind, but I'm not sure if I can trust her with my heart. I have, so far, avoided thinking about her lack of demonstrative affection. I want her to hold me, to kiss me, to say she loves me. But …

"Unghhh," I moan as the big head of her BBC eases its way past the knot of muscle guarding my back entrance.

"Color, pet?" She stops all movement, the head lodged in my opening.

"Yellow." I pant for a few seconds, and then as the wave of pain lifts, I say, "Green."

She grunts her satisfaction and slowly pushes her BBC in further. It isn't long before her hands dig into my hips, adding bruises on top of my bruises. The sensations take me to a floaty place where all I feel is her BBC sliding in and out of my body. The friction is exquisite.

"Oh, yes," my Mistress says with passion. "Fucking yes." I can't believe it. She is going to orgasm as she fucks me in the ass. "Oh, oh, oh," she cries out in passion. She slaps my ass three times, and I realize that she also came last night when the other Mistresses were there. The sound of her cumming sets me off, and it isn't long before my wails combine with hers. She stops pumping and pulls out of me, collapsing on the bed. I start to do the same, but she breathlessly says, "*Table* pose."

I am back up on all fours instantly, knees spread, my cunt and ass pulsing with aftershocks. Remaining open and available in the *Table* pose causes another aftershock to ripple through me.

She catches her breath and sits up. "Go," she commands. "Go kneel on the floor."

I walk backward on my hands and knees until I find the edge of the bed. I somehow scoot off without leaving any more of my wetness on the sheets. I kneel as instructed. "Knees together this time. Hands on your thighs. Palms up."

I do as she instructs and lower my head and keep my eyes down. She stands up in front of me. I hear her take off her BBC and lay it on a towel on her nightstand.

"Good," she praises me. "This is the *Kneel* pose. Pretty self-explanatory, but you'd be surprised how many don't get it right at first." She's probably rolling her eyes or shaking her head. My eyes are down, so I don't know. "Spread your knees so I can see your tribute to me." I slide my knees apart on the carpet, trying not to get a rug burn. I feel the ocean that surges between my thighs.

"Such gorgeous wetness. That's beautiful, pet."

She tousles my hair and says, "Stay like this, so I can see all of you while I get dressed." I hear water running in the bathroom and then closet doors opening. After a while, she finally says, "Look up."

My eyes widen when I see the array of whips and floggers and paddles in her opened armoire. I see ball gags and a whole host of cuffs. There are things in there I don't have names for. I know I shouldn't, but I look over at her and then back to the array of torture equipment. Her chuckle makes me look at her again. She is sporting a grin. One that I can't interpret.

Chapter Seventeen

Submission

"Those are some of the tools of my trade," Mistress Ciara says and nods toward the open armoire full of BDSM paraphernalia. She continues to grin at me. "There is a reason I am showing you these items, but don't worry. They won't be used on you."

I breathe out a slow sigh of relief.

"Pet," she says, "submission is the greatest gift you can give to any Dominant. Submissives must be strong people. You, pet, are very strong to have endured what the other Mistresses and I put you through this weekend. Submissives are not doormats, despite what some people think. There is still so much more for you to learn and to explore." She gestures toward the open armoire.

She looks me in the eye, and I feel as if she wants to say something. In a flash, her expression changes, and she says simply, "Get up. Clean yourself and get dressed." She points to my overnight bag and my folded clothes sitting on her bed. My phone is on top of my clothes. "Meet me downstairs when you're ready." She says this so gently that I know I am in trouble, but not in a you-deserve-a-spanking kind of way. She didn't even give me a time limit. Something is definitely wrong.

"Yes, Mistress," I say but don't move. I wait until she leaves the room, and I no longer hear her on the stairs. My stomach clenches in fear. Something is about to happen. It is already ten o'clock, and I have to be gone by eleven. In a start, I realize that I have not sent my morning messages to Lisa and Miss Olga. I leap to my feet, grab my phone, and send each a short message that says I'm fine and I will be leaving within the hour. I curse when I realize that I have to go back into *Kinks* and send Lisa a secret word. She might call in the cavalry if I don't.

After freshening up in the bathroom and putting on real clothes, which feels incredibly weird after being naked most of the weekend, I grab my bag and take one last look around. I am tempted to take a couple of photos of her bedroom and my pet bed to remember my time here, but I don't. I don't think I should without permission.

My Mistress is sitting on the couch as I come down the stairs. I realize that my breasts and southern region are kind of sore. The nipple Nik bit still aches a little. But I can't think about that right now because the expression on my Mistress's face as she watches me descend the stairs is truly breaking my heart. Despite what she said to me upstairs, maybe I have *not* lived up to her expectations. Maybe she's angry with me.

I drop my bag by the front door to indicate that I know I have to leave. Sadness grips my chest as I realize that my weekend with my Mistress is over. I fly down on my knees in front of her in the *Kneel* position and blurt, "I don't want to leave, Mistress."

"Aww, my Bernadette, but you must. All baby birds must leave the nest sometime." I look up at her, protocols be damned. "I've given you all I can give you, pet. You must move on and find another who can give you what you truly need. I'm not the right one for you."

"No," I say as fear grips my chest alongside the sorrow that is already there. "No, I want you." I fall forward and lean my head on her feet. I grip her ankles. She has every right to kick me off, but she doesn't.

She leans down and pets my head. "Bernadette," she says, "sit up." I do as she asks. Tears are falling down my cheeks. "Listen," she says softly. "I'm glad I got to be your first Mistress and that your first experience wasn't with some bitch poser. I pushed your limits, even your hard limits." She nods her head toward her master bedroom. "Maybe some of those I shouldn't have, but as your Mistress, I knew how to take care of you. I knew how much you could take. Others will not, Bernadette, and that is why you must be able to use your voice. Do you understand me?"

"Yes," I say and look down. My mind whirls at the times I did *not* use my voice and have been stepped on and used. Jen comes to mind first, followed quickly by my department chairman. I look up at Mistress Ciara. I look her full in the eye and say, "Yes, Mistress, I understand. And I *do* understand." I hear the conviction in my voice, and I know she hears it, too.

"Good, because you need to speak up, speak out, and fix whatever isn't working for you," she says firmly. The sternness is gone from her voice; there is only compassionate concern and guidance. "You do have a submissive nature, Bernadette. In fact, you make a glorious submissive, but I do not think for one moment that you are meant to be anyone's slave."

"No?"

"No," she says with a shake of her head. "There is no shame in being a slave, mind you, but you need more. You need to feel the loving, caring arms of your dominant around you and deep kisses and…" She smiles sadly and adds, "And this is more than I can give you." After a moment, she chuckles and says, "Tatiana thinks you need a Mommy figure. She wanted me to tell you that if she didn't have a husband and three kids, she'd scoop you up so fast, your head would spin."

Warmth spreads through my chest at the thought of Mommy Tatiana taking care of me.

"Now, Nik?" Mistress Ciara says, "You don't want to be with him. He has a lot of growing up to do as a Dominant. Believe me, I'm working on him. Last night was a trial run for him, too."

"It was?" My eyes widen. "He is one of your, er, clients?"

"Yes."

"Wow, I had no idea." I am shocked by this revelation. I thought they were all friends. "Mommy Tatiana?"

Mistress Ciara laughs. "No, she's a friend of mine. We've known each other since middle school."

My eyes widen. "Wow."

"I wanted you to have a wide array of experiences," she says. "But now, my dear Bernadette, I must ask you to leave my nest and go free."

I nod and get choked up. I look down, trying to gather my thoughts and get myself back together. My various bruises and sore spots remind me of the amazing adventure I have been on. Part of me wants to beg her to let me come back. To let me pay her, but I already know she will refuse. "Yes, Ma'am," I finally say and then look back up at her.

"Your submission is a gift. Look for a Dominant who is caring and worthy of your trust. And, on the flip side, make sure your Dominant can trust you." She stands up and holds out her hand. I take it and stand up next to her. She pulls me into a quick hug and then looks me in the eye. "Bernadette, I release you from my servitude."

My heart clenches at her words, and I can't help the tears that fall. I take a shaky breath to stop myself from blubbering. I wipe at the stupid tears in my eyes and nod. It's all I can do as I follow her to the front door. I put on my coat and take my bag and keys from her hands. "You have one more task to do for me."

"What's that, Mistress?" I choke out around my tears.

"Send me a message on *Kinks* to let me know you got home all right."

"I will." I feel tears starting again, and I feel like fleeing out her front door, but I don't. I throw myself at her and hug her fiercely. "Thank You, Mistress. I will never forget you." I bolt out the door, knowing she hears the sob that escapes me.

I don't look back.

I manage to keep it together until I am in my car with the door closed and locked. I start the engine and break down in tears. They stream down my face and my chest feels like it's caving in. I have to turn on the heater, but I can't see the buttons. Before I allow myself to operate this heavy machinery, I must get myself together.

I travel through the first four stages of loss several times. I never reach the fifth. She didn't really just break up with me, did she? How the fuck

175

could she do that? It was our first meeting. What if I go back in there and tell her I want more training? I'll be that perfect submissive she says I am. I sigh and wipe at my ever-flowing tears. No, her words were final. Weren't they? Did I really hear them correctly? Why does she think she knows what I need? I could walk back in there, tell her my car won't start, and then just not leave. I sigh as I hear the futility in my words. The truth is she just didn't like me enough. I pull onto the street as depression settles over me. The final stage, acceptance, will be a long time coming, I think, as I get on the highway toward home. I officially love and hate Columbus, Ohio.

I pull in to the first rest stop I see on I-71 South. I don't have to pee; it's just that I'm crying so much that I am having trouble driving. Maybe I need to take a walk in the cold November air to clear my head. I screech into a parking spot and then get out. It is not quite noon, and the day is sunny but bitingly cold. I walk to the far end of the rest area and then back to my car. I have at least stopped crying, but I still feel no better. I figure since I'm here, I might as well use the facilities. With every person I pass, I wonder if they are in a D/s relationship. Is he a submissive? Is she a Dominant? Have they ever heard the words, "I release you from my servitude"? Have they? I head into a stall, hoping I am not about to lose my mind.

Lisa. I have to call her. I have to talk to her about this voice to voice. I hurry up and do my business, wash my hands, and then head back out. I sit on a cold bench in the sun and pull out my phone. I log into *Kinks.com* and message Lisa. I simply type in my phone number and write then a plea.

CRYSTAL_TOY: Call me. Now. Please. Having a breakdown.

Within one minute, my phone rings.

"Lisa?" I say. I can hear the desperation in my voice.

"Yes, yes. Bernadette, are you okay?" she asks.

Oh, her voice is so nice. "She broke up with me. I didn't do anything wrong." The words spill out.

"Oh, honey," Lisa says soothingly. "I'm so sorry this is happening."

"I promise. I didn't do anything wrong. She told me I was a 'glorious submissive,' but that I had to leave the nest."

"She said that?"

"Yessss!" I take a moment to breathe in and then let it out slowly. "I'm sorry, Lisa." I laugh at my apparent mental breakdown. "You're so sweet for calling me back. And so fast, too. It's nice to meet you. Well, meet your voice. You have the sweetest southern accent."

She laughs, and it is a nice sound. "Bernadette, it's nice to meet your voice, too. Now is this a mid-western accent that I'm hearing?"

"More California, I think." I chuckle and then blurt, "What did I do wrong, Lisa?"

"*You* said that *she* said you did nothing wrong," Lisa says. "I think you are simply in sub-frenzy right now. It's something I know well."

"What's sub-frenzy?" I ask.

"All subs go through it, darlin'. Submissives new to the game like you are especially susceptible."

"But what is it?" I stand up and head back to my car. I'm starting to get a chill, and people are looking at me with concern. My tear-stained face is probably giving me away. And I probably look like a lunatic about to spin out of control. It's how I feel anyway.

"Sub-frenzy is basically a drive for connection with a Dominant. You have this desperate need for her attention and her Dominance, and you feel like nothing in your life will work if you can't be with her or at least hear from her and know she loves you and wants you. You feel abandoned and forgotten and unloved if she doesn't pay any attention to you. You feel like you'll do anything just to please her, to get her to notice you, or in your case, to take you back."

"Oh, my God. How the hell did you know all of that was going on in my head? That's exactly how I feel right now." I chuckle and add, "And those were a lot of words you just strung together."

"I've been there. Trust me. And if she broke it off with you, then I'm sure you are frantically trying to figure out why. What did she say exactly?"

I relay what happened that morning to the best of my ability. I even back up the story and tell her everything, and I mean just about everything that happened over the entire weekend.

"Holy shit, Bernadette. What an orgy that was. She's a professional Domme, then?"

"I guess so," I say and turn up the heater.

"That explains it then. In Mistress Ciara's mind, she was training you. Teaching you." Lisa softens her voice when she says, "She was never going to keep you, Bernadette."

"She wasn't?" My heart has just shattered.

"No. You'll replay the events a million times in your head and wonder what you could have done differently –"

"Already been there," I interrupt.

She laughs and says, "And you'll go there again and again, but after a while, you will head into a big down feeling. It's a type of depression. It sounds like you had incredible high highs. Yes?"

"Oh, my God. Yes."

"Those high highs are going to be accompanied by low lows. This is called a sub-drop. So, here's what we're going to do. When you get home later and take a nap –"

"A nap?"

"Yes, I'm ordering you to take a nap. Sub-frenzy is exhausting, dear. So, after your nap, you're going to call me back, and we'll set up a regular time for us to chat. Daily. That means every day, Bernadette."

"Okay. Won't Rachel get mad?" I ask this because the last thing I need is a Dominant ready to kick my ass.

"No, she won't. She's right here, and she's concerned about you, too."

My heart warms a little. "Thank her for me."

"I will. She's seen me in sub-drop often enough to know that it's real, and that it's devastating, but that it's survivable."

"You mean, I'll survive this?" I laugh, but before she can respond, I add, "I can't believe you made me laugh. My world is crashing in on me, and you made me laugh. Thank you."

"You're worth it, lady." I can hear Lisa smile. "Call me once you get home and settled, okay?"

"Yeah, I will." I blow out a sigh. "Thanks again, friend."

Once I hang up with her, I take a deep breath, knowing what I need to do next. A quick text to Jen, and my sights are set on the house I own. Driving to confront Jennifer is a beautiful way to distract me from my misery.

I pull into my former driveway. No, wrong. This is still my driveway. I own it. I owned and lived in the house before Jen moved in with me. Jen is outside, sitting on the front porch step, obviously waiting for me. She is smaller than I remembered her. How is it that this five-foot-two-inch-tall woman was able to rule me for so long? I realize as I see her that I have no feelings of love or affection for her anymore. I did when we first got together, sure, but no more. I look past her and frown at the ton of crap on the front porch. When did she become a slob? I feel sorry for my house. I park and get out of the car.

"I don't have it," Jen says to me. "You can't just show up and demand two-months' rent from me."

"Actually, I can." I am standing at the bottom of the steps, physically lower than she is, but something comes over me. I simply raise one eyebrow and say, "Today is December first. According to the lease you signed, I should have this money today."

"You okay, babe?" comes a voice from the front door.

I almost laugh when I see Jen's 'best friend' Cassidy standing at the front door in babydoll pajamas. Things suddenly become crystal clear to me. I have already been replaced. And then it dawns on me. I had been replaced a long, long time ago. A grin spreads on my face as this part of my life comes into clear focus.

"Yeah," Jen says to her, annoyed. "Go back inside."

Cassidy does as commanded. Part of me wonders if Cassidy is a submissive like me and if Jen has figured out how to be the Dominant her soul seems to want to be. Maybe she needs training from Mistress Ciara. A bite down a laugh. Jen would never survive.

"I think it's time for you to move out," I say to her. "If I don't get this money tomorrow, then I will start eviction proceedings." I have no idea how to evict a tenant, but I'm done getting pushed around. I turn around and head for my still-running car. "You'll have until December fifteenth to get out, and I want the rent that is due."

"You've changed," she says.

I turn around and smile at her. *You have no idea*, I think, and stand up a little taller. Mistress Ciara was right. I am stronger than I realize.

As I head to my car, I already have my phone out, ready to call Professor Wainwright and talk with him about getting the respect in the department that I deserve.

That's right, Mistress Ciara, I am strong, and I have a voice. It's too bad you won't ever hear me use it.

~~~ THE END ~~~

About the Author

Danielle Grainger

Dani is a retired instructor who currently resides in the southeastern USA when she's not travelling the country and putting her newfound freedom to good use. She has always been an avid reader and ventured into writing after reading several novels she felt didn't accurately represent the BDSM lifestyle. With so many rampant misconceptions, she took a chance and crafted admittedly idealized versions of possible experiences. Ever the romantic, Dani hopes not only to entertain her readers but to enlighten and educate them as well.

Dani's Amazon Author Page:
www.amazon.com/stores/Danielle-Grainger

Dani's Facebook:
facebook.com/danielle.grainger.7777

Dani's Instagram:
DaniGrainger84

Dani's Goodreads Page:
www.goodreads.com/author/show/19699760.Danielle_Grainger

Books by Danielle Grainger

THE DENTON HEIGHTS SERIES

The Denton Heights Series is the series that comes BEFORE the Bernadette Series. This group of books tells the stories of the beloved characters who populate the Bernadette Series world and live the BDSM lifestyle. We learn more about the origin stories of Madison and Shasti; Jaleesa, Tina, Harriet, Dana, DeShawn, and Kari; Rowena and Minjung; and Rikki. Victoria (AKA Daddy Vic), Lydia, and Brittany also feature in this series. The Denton Heights Series is basically the "Prequel Series" to the Bernadette Series.

Under Her Wing (Denton Heights Book 1)
(The Shasti and Madison Story)
An age-gap lesbian erotic romance with consensual light BDSM aspects featuring *littles*.
* 2023 Finalist in the Golden Crown Literary Society Awards *

Madison Kim finds herself on a bus bound for Denton Heights, Ohio, a Cincinnati suburb. Her mother sent her there without notice to care for an elderly Korean woman Madison had never met. Madison is twenty-two-and-three-quarters years old and has a high school diploma, but she isn't smart enough to go to college...so they tell her. Now, she spends her time caring for Mrs. Park, going to the beloved Cincinnati Zoo, and watching movies on her outdated phone. She's not really sure why she's there, but she's taking it day by day.

Then, she meets strong, nurturing Miss Shasti at a tea dance.

Shasti Balakrishnan has been looking for someone to call hers for more years than she cares to count. She wants a woman to love and care for in a nurturing Mommy Domme/*little-girl* scenario. She's thirty-two and already a partner in a thriving medical clinic in Denton Heights, but truth be told – she's lonely. She thought she'd found a companion in Amber back in D.C., but that fizzled out once they realized they weren't what each other wanted—or needed.

And then she meets adorably precocious Madison at a tea dance.

ISBN: 978-1-953734-10-5 (e-Book)
ISBN: 978-1-953734-13-6 (Paperback)

In Her Cage (Denton Heights Book 2)

(The Jaleesa and Tina Story)

A lesbian interracial erotic romance with consensual light BDSM aspects.

Jaleesa Whitmore is a lesbian Domme in and out of fast relationships fueled by sex. She didn't understand addiction. Not yet, anyway. Although she had been almost one full year sober, she was done with it. She was moments from heading down the familiar road of drinking that always made her feel good and filled that void. She was about to get her life back on its old track when a fateful encounter with a stranger, who would become a trusted friend, halted her downslide. She didn't know it then, but this encounter would not only lead her to a series of events and people that would change how she looked at life, but also how she approached it.

Tina Jenkins likes women but is asexual and afraid to try for another relationship. She does understand addiction. Just shy of eleven years clean of her opioid addiction following a dental procedure right out of high school, her parents carefully constructed and monitored everything in her world. It didn't matter that she was thirty-one years old and still living in the pink bedroom in her parents' house. It didn't matter that her mother now had to work from home and that her parents had to track her location and conduct routine searches of her bag, car, computer, phone, and room. None of it mattered because she was clean.

And then asexual Tina meets promiscuous Jaleesa. And everything changed for both of them.

ISBN: 978-1-953734-28-0 (e-Book)
ISBN: 978-1-953734-29-7 (Paperback)

Within Her Grasp (Denton Heights Book 3)

(The Marta and Shanice Story)

A lesbian age gap interracial erotic romance with consensual light BDSM aspects.

"Within Her Grasp" is an age-gap interracial lesbian romance that tells the tale of two women who had settled for unhappy lives. And then they meet.

White, thirty-something Marta Ingersoll was done with people. She just wanted to be left alone at work and at home, thank you. Her inside cat and the outside stray were all she needed. And her sister, Nora, too, of course. But that was it. And then, one fateful afternoon, her instincts to save a woman in obvious distress kicked in, and her life was shoved onto a strange new course.

Black, twenty-something Shanice Ward never got a break. Life had thrown challenge after challenge at the young woman, and this latest thing was too much, but it wouldn't stop. Woken up from a sound sleep by someone trying to remove her clothing, she shrieked for him to leave her alone. He didn't, but then, the most amazing thing happened. She discovered that superheroes were real, and one had just flown into her room to save her, and her life was shoved onto a strange new course.

ISBN: 978-1-953734-30-3 (e-Book)
ISBN: 978-1-953734-31-0 (Paperback)

By Her Command (Denton Heights Book 4)
(The Rowena and Minjung Story)
A lesbian interracial erotic romance with consensual BDSM aspects.

"By Her Command" is an erotic interracial lesbian romance containing consensual aspects of BDSM. It finds Rowena Tate in need of a submissive who can also manage her household. It's also the tale of Minjung Lee, who is desperate to find a Domme so she won't find herself homeless again. Trust does not come easily for either of them.

Rowena is a white Domme in her late thirties. Through experience, she has come to believe that most, if not all, submissives are selfish creatures who only want what she can provide without considering the person behind the flogger and the paycheck.

Minjung is an East Asian submissive in her mid-thirties. Through experience, she has come to believe that most, if not all, Dominants are selfish creatures who go well beyond contracted limits because there is no one to tell them not to.

Despite their reservations, both are told by members of the Denton Heights BDSM community that they are a good match and lucky to have found each other. Rowena isn't so sure. Neither is Minjung. Time will tell, won't it?

ISBN: 978-1-953734-32-7 (e-Book)
ISBN: 978-1-953734-33-4 (Paperback)

Toward Her Passion (Denton Heights Book 5)
(A Rikki Carmichael Story)
A lesbian erotic reminiscence with consensual BDSM aspects

Rikki Carmichael is strong, stoic, and in charge. She does *not* need help from anyone. She can navigate her own life, thank you very much, and resents her friends' efforts to give her charity. She doesn't take charity; she gives it. Financial troubles threaten to topple her coffee shop business, her livelihood, and her sense of self-worth. Abruptly single and oddly uninterested in finding a new relationship, be it a long-term life partner or a short-term lover, she finds herself reminiscing about past loves and relationships: Hard Eileen, fun Emily, newbie Sarah, and young Jessica.

The anniversary of her mother's death all those years ago sends her into another bout of 'deep downs,' the code words her mother used for Rikki's bouts with depression growing up. Her bestie, Shasti, advises her to make room for someone, a new lover, or a life partner. Shasti wants Rikki to send a message to the universe that she is ready to receive someone into her life. And, lo and behold, in walks Esme, a blonde bombshell customer at the coffee shop. Rikki's hopes are lifted...until they aren't. With no biological family left to lean on, Rikki has to find the strength to become vulnerable and ask for help. Easier said than done. It's much easier to counsel others than to ask for help for herself. She discovers, however, that asking for help is where real strength lies.

ISBN: 978-1-953734-40-2 (e-Book)
ISBN: 978-1-953734-41-9 (Paperback

THE BERNADETTE SERIES

Dr. Bernadette Garneau holds a Ph.D. in Mathematics and has just gotten out of a four-year relationship. Shortly after the breakup, she began an exploration of her repressed sexual desires. One message from a beautiful and powerful online Mistress and Bernadette leaps into the world of BDSM. The Mistress takes charge, and Bernadette reels in the heady power this stranger has over her. She has gotten a taste of the life, and she wants more. She needs more. Several online and in-person experiences with BDSM and Power Exchange have led to cravings she doesn't quite understand. A brief sexual exchange with an online Goddess unleashes an incredible pain-to-pleasure connection that she hadn't understood before. As she sifts through the posers and one-night stands, she homes in on what her submissive nature needs from a Domme. The Bernadette Series follows Bernadette's journey into the world of BDSM and her search for love and sexual satisfaction. As she said, "I want a monogamous partner who wants to not only love and nurture me but who also wants to drape me over her lovely couch and have her way with me."

Wrecking Bernadette
(Book One in the Bernadette Series)
A lesbian's exploration of her sexuality with consensual aspects of BDSM.

Dr. Bernadette Garneau holds a Ph.D. in Mathematics and has been out of a four-year relationship for four months. One good thing about breaking up is that Bernadette is free to explore her repressed sexual desires. One message from a beautiful and powerful online Mistress, and Bernadette leaps into the world of BDSM. Mistress Ciara takes charge, and Bernadette reels in the heady power this stranger has over her. She has gotten a taste of the *life*, and she wants more. She *needs* more.

ISBN: 978-1-953734-00-6 (e-Book)
ISBN: 978-1-953734-14-3 (Paperback)

(S)mothering Bernadette

(Book Two in the Bernadette Series)

A lesbian's continuing exploration of her sexuality with aspects of BDSM.

Dr. Bernadette Garneau's universe is pushing her toward change. Her initial experiences with BDSM and Power Exchange have led to cravings she doesn't quite understand. A brief sexual exchange with an online Goddess unleashes an incredible pain-to-pleasure connection she hadn't understood until that encounter. But after sleeping on it, she clearly understands that this Goddess would never be the long-term relationship she sought.

Disappointed, she wonders if she should just give up and move back to California to be closer to her family. That is, until she meets Mama_Luvs, an online Mommy Domme. The woman is nurturing yet stern from the start and is just … perfect. And then Mama_Luvs wants to meet. Starry-eyed Bernadette packs for a New Year's Eve weekend, hoping that this time she's found *the one* – the one who wants to love and nurture her but who also wants to drape her over a couch and have her way with her.

ISBN: 978-1-953734-01-3 (e-Book)
ISBN: 978-1-953734-15-0 (Paperback)

Becoming Bernadette
(Book Three in the Bernadette Series)
A lesbian erotic romance with light consensual BDSM aspects.

University professor Dr. Bernadette Garneau has fallen in love with the world of BDSM. She has a nascent interest in the pain-to-pleasure connection, but she has yet to find partners interested in nurturing the soul within her body that they play with. Admittedly, she's had incredible sexual encounters with experienced Dommes, but all of them left her feeling cold for whatever reason. Most of them simply wanted a sadistic roll in the hay. Bernadette wants a strong Domme who will love and nurture her before flogging her on a St. Andrew's cross and afterward when her body is spent.

One afternoon, she finally musters the courage to venture out and meet some new friends in the local BDSM community. In walks a tall, handsome butch woman with fantastic hair and a confident stride. When this woman asks Bernadette, "Are you collared?" Bernadette truthfully answers, "No," and accepts a dinner invitation for that very evening. She is walking on stars when she gets home at 2 a.m. after an ethereal sexual liaison. On the one hand, she wonders who she is becoming – she's never been this promiscuous. And on the other hand, she wonders if this strong butch woman could finally be the Domme of her dreams.

ISBN: 978-1-953734-02-0 (e-Book)
ISBN: 978-1-953734-12-9 (Paperback)

Desiring Bernadette
(Book Four in the Bernadette Series)
A lesbian erotic romance with light consensual BDSM aspects.

*** 2022 Finalist in the Golden Crown Literary Society Awards ***

Rikki Carmichael finally feels that deep D/s relationship she has been craving since her Aunt Tilda introduced her to *the life*. She embraced her dominant side early on, but finding a suitable submissive woman who wanted more than a quick roll in the dungeon proved elusive. That is, until Professor Bernadette Garneau arrived on the scene. Now collared and committed to Rikki, will Bernadette prove to be different, or will she turn out like all the others — fickle and full of lies and deception?

And will this perfect sub stay with her when she realizes Rikki's ship is sinking? She'd almost lost the coffee shop she owns when creditors came knocking down her door en masse, seeking payment for debts that weren't hers. Rikki managed to keep her staff and most of her friends in the dark about it, but she has not been able to get out from under it. With high stakes all around, Rikki looks for the peace she seeks within her relationship with Bernadette. If this one fails, it may be time to leave the *life* entirely and go live in a cabin somewhere isolated in the woods. But buying a cabin takes money – money she just doesn't have.

ISBN: 978-1-953734-03-7 (e-Book)
ISBN: 978-1-953734-09-9 (Paperback)

Loving Bernadette
(Book Five in the Bernadette Series)
A lesbian erotic romance with light consensual BDSM aspects.

Bernadette Garneau, a beloved professor of mathematics, is a natural submissive. She likes structure and rules and finally found a way of life and a woman who would provide them. The BDSM community she stumbled upon in Denton Heights, Ohio, is where she found Rikki Carmichael, now her dominant partner and fiancée. Rikki is everything she's dreamed of. Yes, Bernadette found the captain of her ship. With Rikki's support and guidance, maybe other parts of her life can finally come together, too – like the respect she deserves but hasn't gotten at the university. Why won't anyone see that she deserves to teach those upper-level courses? And to move out of her closet of an office? What do they know that she does not?

Rikki Carmichael, the respected owner of Rikki's Coffee Shop in town, has finally found the woman of her dreams in super-smart and super-real Bernadette Garneau. Bernadette is a submissive who instinctively knows how to take care of Rikki and accepts Rikki's need to be in charge. Bernadette is the first submissive Rikki's ever had that wasn't solely out for her own gain. Once Rikki can climb out of the deep financial debt she's found herself in, she will finally make their engagement to be married public.

Miscommunication, faulty assumptions, and unmet expectations threaten this union seemingly made in heaven. When life comes at them hard and fast, they must rely on their bond and their loving, self-made family of friends.

ISBN: 978-1-953734-08-2 (e-Book)
ISBN: 978-1-953734-11-2 (Paperback)

www.ingramcontent.com/pod-product-compliance
Lightning Source LLC
Chambersburg PA
CBHW071204260626
47162CB00003B/1166